Preacher

Books in the
Jonas Series

Book 1
Runaway Buggy

Book 2
Hitched

Book 3
Preacher

Book 4
Becca

Book 3 ❖ *Jonas Series*

Preacher

Carol Duerksen & Maynard Knepp

Illustrations by Susan Bartel

WILLOWSPRING DOWNS

Preacher
Book 3 — Jonas Series
Copyright © 1996 by WillowSpring Downs

Second Printing, 2002

Printed in the United States of America

Cover and Story Illustrations by Susan Bartel
Page design & layout by C:PROMPT Creations
Hillsboro, Kansas

This story is a fictional account of an Amish family. Names, characters, places and incidents are either imaginary or are used fictitiously, and their resemblance, if any, to real persons, living or dead, is purely coincidental.

Library of Congress Catalog Number 96-61387
ISBN 0-9648525-2-7

Welcome to the Jonas Series!

It began with a dream. A "what if…" A "Suppose we write…" It began with the interest friends and family expressed in Maynard's Amish background. He'd tell stories. They'd listen spellbound. And we'd go home wondering, "Wouldn't it be fun to write a book?"

So, after years of saying it, we finally put some action behind our words. Carol had come across a quote somewhere that said, "If you're going to run with the big dogs, you've got to get off the porch." We decided to get off the porch and write that book. *Runaway Buggy* was conceived.

The delivery of *Runaway Buggy* took place under the expertise of another entrepreneurial Hillsboro business called C:Prompt Creations. They took our manuscript and made it look like a book. And they suggested we call *Runaway Buggy* "Book 1 of the Jonas Series." That sounded pretty neat to us, so we did.

Runaway Buggy was released in October, 1995, and six weeks later we realized we'd better do a second printing. We also decided to write Book 2 in the Jonas Series, because it appeared that people who'd met our fictional character, Jonas Bontrager, in *Runaway Buggy* wanted to read more. Jonas's life continued in *Hitched*, which was released in August of 1996.

You're now holding the third book in the series in your hand. Carol's always loved horses, so she couldn't resist the opportunity to incorporate that interest into *Preacher*. In fact, the pasture that is a part of our WillowSpring Downs farm is home for three horses, one of them a big black quarter horse gelding named Spud Webb. But that's another story.

What's next in the Jonas Series? *Becca*. God willing, we plan for that to be out in spring, 1997. We have two more books in mind for the series, and other ideas floating around too. This dreaming thing, and working to make the dreams come true, can get addictive.

But in all honesty, the dream would have stopped at *Runaway Buggy* if it weren't for you and other readers like you. You bought the book, read it, and encouraged us to keep going. Your support means everything. As long as you want to read what we write, we'll do our best to keep up our end of the deal. Thanks a lot for helping make the Jonas Series dream-in-process come true!

Carol Duerksen & Maynard Knepp

Contents

Chapter 1

The Foaling

Jonas Bontrager had told himself he had to wake up in several hours when he went to bed that night. Patsy was close, and what with the full moon and all, this could be the night. So, when his internal clock prodded him awake sometime after midnight, he slipped out of bed.

The full moon shining through the window illuminated the room enough for him to put on his shirt and barn-door pants. His wife, Sue Ann, stirred and muttered sleepily, "Let me know, honey." Jonas bent down and kissed her cheek. "I will. I'll be right back."

Normally, Jonas would have needed a flashlight to navigate his way through their home at night, but the moonlight filled in quite nicely. He slipped his bare feet into a pair of work shoes standing next to the back door, and stepped outside.

May was Jonas's favorite month in Kansas. Spring rains and the natural cycle of life were turning the world lush and green. This second night of May, a cool breeze played softly in the newborn leaves on the cottonwood trees near their house. He smiled at the sound of the tinkling leaves as he searched the moon shadows for the tall thoroughbred mare.

Patsy stood uneasily near one of the trees, and as Jonas walked toward the fence separating them, she folded herself to the ground heavily. Jonas let himself through the gate.

"Hey, Patsy, is it time?" he addressed her quietly. "You okay, girl?"

The mare studied Jonas with liquid brown eyes, but she seemed preoccupied. Standing up, she took a few steps, circled twice, and went down again.

Jonas didn't need to see any more.

"Sue Ann!" he exclaimed, sitting on the bed next to his wife moments later. "If you want to see it, get dressed and come out! Hurry!"

Then he was gone again.

Jonas could feel his heart racing, partly from the sprint into the house and back, and partly from anticipation. They'd been waiting 11 months for this. Patsy's foal was about to be born.

In fact, during the few minutes he'd been gone, a nose and two tiny hooves had emerged. Patsy struggled with another contraction, but nothing happened. She stood up, desperate to move the foal out. Jonas hated this part. The waiting. He wanted to help. He wanted that baby out, breathing, on the ground. This waiting made him so nervous.

"Is it coming?" Sue Ann asked as she walked cautiously through the gate and toward Jonas. Her waist-length dark-brown hair and chocolate eyes shone in the moonlight. "Is everything okay?"

"I think so," Jonas answered, his eyes shifting from Sue Ann back to the agitated mare. "She's done this before, and it's coming right. I don't think it'll be long."

Even as Jonas spoke, Patsy dropped to the ground again. She grunted as a powerful labor pain overtook her body, and then the foal's head and shoulders were out. Another quick push, and the baby lay on the grass less than 15 feet from where Jonas crouched. The wet, black body moved, and Jonas couldn't resist. He slipped up to its head and quickly cleared the mucous from its nose. "Good girl, Patsy," Jonas soothed. "Good girl!"

Patsy stood up and turned to nuzzle the newborn. Her soft lips began at the foal's head—greeting, stimulating, and drying all at the same time. She nickered low and soft. The foal shook his head.

"He's completely black!" Sue Ann exclaimed. "He's beautiful!"

"*He?*" Jonas glanced quizzically at his wife. "Do you know something I don't?"

"No," Sue Ann answered. "I guess we'll have to wait until he—she—stands up."

The youngster had it in mind already, but his body didn't quite understand—especially the legs. Those long, spindly legs that had been folded for so long—now they were supposed to coordinate themselves into a standing position? No way. Or so it seemed to the young Amish couple watching the colt. By the time he got all four legs straightened out and planted precariously on the ground, one would give way. Then he'd gather himself together and try again. Jonas stood close behind Sue Ann and wrapped his arms around her waist as they waited. The colt's black coat shone in the brightness of the moon.

"Midnight. We could call him Midnight," Sue Ann murmured.

"It fits," Jonas agreed. "And you're right about it being a boy. I can see, now that he's up on his feet."

Jonas had no more said it than the foal lost his tenuous balance and buckled back down to the ground.

"He looks like those little toys where you push the bottom and the whole thing collapses in a pile," Sue Ann giggled. "You know what I mean?"

"Yeah," Jonas agreed. "But he'll figure it out, and by morning, he'll be running."

"I can hardly wait for the children to see him," Sue Ann caressed the arms holding her, and lifted her face to meet Jonas's. "Becca's been asking every day when Patsy's going to have her baby, and Lydianne will just squeal."

Chapter 1

"Yeah, we'll show them in the morning," Jonas kissed the back of Sue Ann's neck. "Let's get back to bed. Morning isn't that far away."

Jonas couldn't help but smile contentedly to himself as he and Sue Ann walked arm-in-arm to their house. Such a gorgeous spring night in Kansas, a fine new foal, two adorable little girls sleeping inside, and beside him—beside him a woman that filled his heart, mind, and body with pleasure. Yes, life was good. Very, very good.

❖ ❖ ❖

As predicted, two-year-old Lydianne squealed with delight as she peaked through the fence early that morning. The new colt was nursing, his short bushy tail waving with satisfaction. "Huchley! Huchley!" Lydianne repeated, pointing a chubby finger at the horses.

"Yes, Lydianne, it's a baby colt!" Sue Ann agreed, holding her daughter's other hand. "You like the baby?"

"I like him a lot," Becca answered the question addressed to her sister. "What's his name?"

"We're not sure," Jonas stood beside his five-year-old daughter. "Mommy and I talked about Midnight, since he's so black and he was born around midnight. Do you like that name?"

"It's okay. But why is he black, when his mommy's brown?"

"Maybe his daddy is black," Jonas answered.

"Where's his daddy?"

"He's far away, in Indiana."

"Why?"

"Because that's where he lives. Patsy came from Indiana too."

"Did you go to Inji anna to get her?"

"No, I bought her at a sale. I thought she was a beautiful mare, and when they said she was going to have a baby, I couldn't help myself. I bought her."

"Oh," Becca paused. "Can Ben and Marie come see him after school?"

"Sure! And speaking of school, young lady, you need to be getting ready. Race you to the house!" Jonas challenged. He waited a second for Becca to take off, then sprinted behind her. "Me too! Me too!" Lydianne cried, dropping her mother's hand and toddling after her father and sister. Sue Ann quickly followed her family into the plain yet attractive white house. If they didn't hurry, Becca would miss her school bus.

❖ ❖ ❖

Ben and Marie Jacobs lived just down the road from Jonas and Sue Ann, and they often got off the school bus at the Bontragers. With both of their parents working, the children could either be at home alone for about an hour or hang out at the Bontragers. Ben was six, so he and Becca usually played together. At ten, Marie helped entertain Lydianne, played with Ben and Becca, or sometimes helped Sue Ann around the house.

One of the things that Jonas found fascinating and somewhat ironic was the interest Ben and Marie had in being with his family. The Jacobs weren't Amish. In Amish terminology, they were "English" people; in this case, they happened to be Catholic. At home, Ben and Marie had videos, games, a computer—all kinds of "worldly" toys and things to do. They didn't have any of those options at the Bontragers. A sandpile, swing set, a few dolls, other "old-fashioned" toys, some cats and a dog—that's what kept his children and Ben and Marie entertained. They didn't seem to mind either. In fact, they complained when they had to go home.

Today, when Cindy Jacobs stopped by to pick up her children, neither was ready to go home. For one thing, they wanted to get closer to the colt, and Sue Ann had said that had to wait until Jonas came home from his job at the Schmidt dairy. For another thing, Becca'd been begging for a picnic outside, and when Sue Ann agreed, Ben and Marie wouldn't hear of leaving. They wanted to be in on the picnic. So Sue Ann had said "Sure, they can stay, and Jonas can run them home in the buggy later on in the evening."

Jonas drove the Schmidt dairy pickup into his yard shortly after 7:00 p.m., and he'd barely stepped out of the cab before he was swamped by four eager children. "Ben wants to touch the colt!" Becca said, grabbing her dad's hand. "Can he? Can you help us?"

"Huchley! Huchley!" Lydianne prattled in Dutch, reaching for her father's other hand. "Go! Go!"

Laughing, Jonas allowed himself to be led toward the white corral fence. "So what do you think of our new young'un?" he addressed Marie, who'd been more restrained but whose interest shone in her eyes.

"I think he's wonderful," she responded. "It's funny, but he reminds me of a priest."

"A priest?" Jonas wondered. "Why?"

"Well, because he's wearing black, except for that little white spot on his neck."

"White on his neck? I don't remember seeing that," Jonas said as the little group reached the fence.

"It's there. See?" Marie pointed.

Jonas instructed the children to stay outside the fence while he went in. "Easy, girl, easy," he spoke softly to the mare. "Can we see the little guy for a minute?"

As he neared Patsy, he dropped to a crouch and stopped. Slowly he reached out to the colt and began scratching the side of its neck. His soothing voice continued.

"Hey, little guy, how're you doing? Does this feel good?"

Obviously it did. The colt stood very still. Whoever or whatever this was, was smaller than him, and the neck scratching felt good.

Jonas continued working his hands along the colt's body until he had one arm around his narrow chest and one around his slender rump. "Okay, Ben and Marie. You can come in, but walk slowly and be very quiet," he instructed.

The Jacobs children entered the pen and approached Jonas and the colt in awe. Surprised, the colt tried to jump, but Jonas had a firm hold on him. Patsy nickered nervously and sniffed the colt and Jonas. "It's okay, Patsy, it's okay," Jonas reassured.

The first visit to the colt was short, but all of the children, even little Lydianne, got to pet him. It wasn't until they were all standing outside the pen again that Jonas responded to Marie's observation.

"You're right, he does have a few white hairs on the front of his neck," he said. "I guess you mean that looks like a priest's collar."

"What's a priest?" Becca asked.

"In Marie and Ben's church, a priest is like a preacher."

"Preacher! You should call him Preacher!" Ben piped up. "Come 'ere, Preacher!"

"Peecher! Peecher!" Lydianne chimed in.

"His name's Midnight, isn't it, Dad?" Becca wondered.

"Well, I think so. I suppose he could be Midnight Preacher," Jonas conceded.

"Well, I'm going to call him Preacher!" Ben stated.

"Peecher!" Lydianne pointed at the black colt watching them from the security of his mother's side.

Chapter 2

No Fear

From the day Preacher was born, the Jacobs children rarely missed their after-school stop at the Bontrager home. Along with Becca, they'd pester Sue Ann until she went along with them to see the colt. Preacher never knew any fear of these two-legged creatures, because they'd been a part of his world from the moment of his birth. Sure, he saw less of them than he did his dam, but they seemed to keep showing up. And so far, it had never been unpleasant to have them around.

"Okay, little guy, let's try this on for size," Jonas crooned to Preacher one evening when he was several days old. An audience of five—Sue Ann and the Bontrager and Jacobs children—watched as Jonas deftly slipped a tiny blue halter over the colt's nose and behind his ears. The colt shook his head, but before he could get rid of the strange thing on his face, Jonas had it buckled on his neck. "Feels funny, huh?" Jonas scratched Preacher on the neck—that special place where it felt so good. The colt's lips moved in pleasure, and Jonas caressed the soft whiskers under Preacher's chin.

"Look, he's got a little beard," he chuckled. "See?"

The children stepped closer for a better look.

"That must be because he's an Amish colt," Marie remarked, and Jonas laughed out loud. The sudden outburst made the colt jump, which in turn scared little Lydianne. She retreated quickly to the safety of her mother's skirts, but

the other three children weren't as easily discouraged.

"We want to play with him," Ben said.

"We've been out here every day. He likes us," Becca added.

"It's good for him to be getting used to you," Jonas agreed. "But you have to be careful. You saw how he got scared when I laughed. Sometimes a colt will kick if he's scared. You have to watch out for that." Jonas had eased up to Preacher again, and this time was holding him lightly by the halter. As long as Jonas scratched and rubbed him, he didn't seem to mind. Jonas unbuckled the halter and slipped it off again.

"We won't scare him," Marie promised. "We'll always be nice to him."

"I know you will," Jonas agreed. "The other thing you need to know is that when a colt is playing, and having fun, he'll sometimes kick up his heels. Just out of silliness, you know? But even if he's having fun, if you're in the way of his hooves, it could hurt you real bad." Jonas picked up the colt's legs, one by one. "I'm doing this so he gets used to it, because when he gets older, he'll need to have shoes put on him. But I don't want any of you kids picking up his legs like this. Understand?"

Jonas looked at each of the children, and they all nodded solemnly.

"Peecher," Lydianne said, her courage back. "Me touch." She toddled from Sue Ann toward Jonas.

Kneeling on one knee, Jonas took his youngest daughter in one arm while he continued soothing the colt with the other. "Here, you can pet him," he said, and Lydianne's bright blue eyes sparkled with delight as her little fingers stroked the shiny black coat. "Pi-ty!" she said almost reverently. "Pi-ty Peecher!"

❖ ❖ ❖

The first Sunday in July found the Bontrager family

going to Jonas's parents, Fred and Esther Bontrager, for church. The Amish held their worship services in their homes, taking turns amongst themselves throughout the year. "Having church" meant weeks of preparation and cleaning. Esther's family, including Sue Ann, had spent several days helping her clean the house from top to bottom. Nothing was left untouched. The barn got its own thorough going-over, because that's where the men would hang out before and after the service.

Chapter
2

"It's not so bad, for July," Jonas remarked as they rode down the sandy Kansas road behind the clop-clop-clop of the family horse, Lightning. "The clouds might keep it from getting so hot."

"That'd be nice," Sue Ann remarked. "I'm not sure I'm up to sitting in a horribly stuffy house for three hours this morning."

Jonas glanced at his wife on the seat next to him in the open hack buggy. "What's the matter? You're not feeling good?" Jonas quizzed.

Sue Ann looked at their girls in the wagon bed behind them. Unlike their English counterparts, who would be strapped into car seat belts for their safety, the young Amish girls had "free rein" in the back of the buggy. A serious game of "church" with their dolls was in process. Becca was busy explaining that the dolls needed to be taken out of church to have their diapers changed.

"No, I'm not." Sue Ann answered Jonas. "I haven't been for the last month or so," She laid her hand on Jonas's leg, and her dark eyes sought his under the black broad-brimmed hat.

"You don't mean … are you?" Jonas's blue eyes acknowledged what hers were trying to say.

Sue Ann nodded, a smile now greeting his.

"How far?" Jonas wondered, suddenly feeling the need to whisper.

"I figure two months."

Jonas was quiet for a moment, and then the chuckle building inside him spilled out into the Kansas countryside.

"Quiet, Daddy!" Becca admonished from behind them. "We're having church!"

"Sorry, Becca," Jonas apologized, trying to be serious, but one look at Sue Ann brought the laughter back.

"The night Preacher was born," he said.

Sue Ann couldn't resist his contagious mirth, and she giggled too. "I've been thinking, we could call him—or her—something like 'Moon.'"

Jonas laughed again, a contented, happy sound. He put his arm around his wife and kissed her on the cheek. "I'm pulling for a boy," he said.

❖ ❖ ❖

Arriving at his parents' farm, Jonas dropped Sue Ann and the girls off at the house and then drove Lightning to the hedgerow that bordered the north side of the farm. He unhitched Lightning from the buggy, then tied him up to a tree. Several dozen other horses and buggies were scattered around the yard, and more were still arriving.

Jonas approached the circle of men standing near the barn, talking and exchanging the latest news and gossip. They were all dressed in basically identical black pants, white pocketless shirts, black vests, and black hats. He went around the circle and shook hands with each man, then joined the group.

At approximately 9:30, the men began moving toward the house, and then filed into the living and dining room area, where rows of gray backless benches awaited them. The women and children were already seated in the kitchen and two bedrooms opening up into the living area. After the men were seated, a long row of benches remained empty. Jonas watched as the ritual of "bringing in the boys" played out in front of the congregation. The boys, ages approximately 12 to 15, had waited outside as long as possible, until one of the ministers summoned them. Now they too filed into their spots.

Jonas found Sue Ann in the sea of white-capped faces. Lydianne was on her lap, and Becca beside her. Sue Ann looked flushed, and Jonas hoped she'd be okay. It was bad enough if she didn't feel well. Having two squirmy girls to take care of didn't help.

Jonas kept his eye on Sue Ann and the girls as the service began. Halfway through the second song, she stood up and made her way out, girls in tow. Every eye seemed to be on her, Jonas noted, and he felt so embarrassed for Sue Ann. Leaving the worship with children wasn't unusual—doing it that early in the service was. And from the look on her face, Sue Ann wasn't going out because of the girls.

From his place in the living room, Jonas could discreetly see outside, and his view included the outdoor toilet. Sue Ann was headed that way.

When Sue Ann returned, the bishop, who happened to be her grandfather, Moses Eash, was preaching. At 80, Mose, as he was known, had been the bishop for as long as Jonas could remember. In fact, Mose had been chosen as a minister in The Lot when he was in his early 20's, when Sue Ann's father, Cris, was just a baby. The Lot fell on him again when he was 45, and he became bishop. For nearly 60 years, Mose had been preaching to the congregation, and never had a sermon outline before him. It wasn't allowed. The Amish believed in the "inspired message from God," just as they believed in choosing their leadership through the drawing of The Lot. Jonas knew, from conversations with non-Amish Christians such as his boss, that outsiders didn't understand this "chance" method of choosing ministers, and then not allowing them to preach with notes. But that's the way it had always been done.

Jonas stood up and met Sue Ann and the girls before they sat down again. He silently took the girls with him and returned to his seat.

Chapter 2

Mose preached for about an hour, and then another minister took his turn. Despite the overcast sky, the air in the house grew hot and stuffy as the temperature outdoors climbed. Having more than a hundred bodies seated close together didn't help the situation.

"Daddy!" Becca whispered loudly beside Jonas. "When are the cookies coming?"

"Pretty soon," Jonas answered, hoping it was true.

It seemed like a long time, but finally the bowl of large "church cookies" worked its way down Jonas's row. Tempting as it was for the adults to help themselves, the cookies were for children only. Lydianne, who'd been half-asleep on Jonas's lap, woke up in time to grab one. Becca tried for two, but Jonas said no.

After nearly three hours of sermons, singing, and responses to the sermons, the church service was over. Quietly, yet eagerly, the congregation spilled outside. They'd be back in the house for the noon meal together soon, but first, they needed to stretch and get fresh air.

❖ ❖ ❖

Jonas, Sue Ann, and the girls returned home later that afternoon. Jonas knew the moment Lightning turned into the yard that something was wrong. Patsy was pacing the fence, whinnying frantically. Preacher was nowhere to be seen.

About that time, a frightened scream came from behind the house, and suddenly a long-legged black body streaked past them, a long white rope dragging behind in the dirt.

Jonas tossed Lightning's reins to Sue Ann, then jumped down from the buggy and sprinted toward what was now cries of pain.

Ben Jacobs was sitting on the ground, sobbing loudly, while his sister Marie tried desperately to comfort him.

"What happened?" Jonas bent down toward Ben. "Marie! What happened?!"

"Preacher kicked Ben!" she said, on the verge of tears herself. Guilt and terror streaked her usually calm, serene face. "Is he okay? Is Ben okay?"

Jonas was relieved to see that it was his arm that Ben was clutching. At least he hadn't been hit in the head.

"Ben," he said, trying to quiet the youngster, "let me see your arm."

"What happened?" Sue Ann and the girls rushed up.

"They must have had Preacher out here, for some reason. He kicked Ben—I think in his arm."

"Let me see," Sue Ann stooped down. "Where does it hurt, Ben?"

Ben's sobs had slowed down, but he continued to hold his upper left arm with his right hand.

"Here," he choked.

Sue Ann inspected the arm. "I don't think it's broken— just bruised," she said, helping Ben stand up. "Let's go inside and put some ice on it."

Sue Ann took the children in the house while Jonas worked at getting Preacher and his mother back together. Both horses were frantically running on opposite sides of the white fence. Jonas caught the worried mare and led her outside the corral. After the reunion with her colt, Patsy followed Jonas back into the pen, Preacher close at her side.

"So, tell me how this all came about," Jonas questioned the Jacobs children as they sipped glasses of Kool-aid at the Bontrager table a few moments later.

"We walked down here because we wanted to play with Preacher," Ben said.

"We were just scratching him by the gate," Marie continued. "Then Ben said we should put his lead rope on, like you do, and lead him out of the gate."

"So we did," Ben admitted.

"But then he freaked out. He sorta jumped and kicked. He tore the rope out of my hands and started running," Marie said. "My hands really hurt," she admitted.

Jonas took one look at the young girl's hands and could see the rope burn. "You've got to put some aloe vera on that," he said to Marie. "Sue Ann has a plant. It'll help take the burning out," he paused. "You kids are lucky, you know it? That kick from Preacher could have hit Ben in the head. Don't you know better than to play with him when we aren't around?"

Marie and Ben both nodded.

"I'll take you home now," Jonas said, and walked out to where Sue Ann had left Lightning tied to the hitching post. He trembled to think how bad Ben's injury could have been.

Chapter 3
E.J.

Nine months after the birth of Preacher, it was Jonas's turn to be awakened by Sue Ann in the middle of a cold night in late January.

"Jonas!" she shook the shoulders of her husband under the heavy comforter. "Wake up! I think you should go get the Jacobs."

Jonas had been sleeping lightly for the past week, aware that Sue Ann might be uttering just those words at any time.

"You sure?" he asked, already out of bed and half dressed.

"I think so. Hurry! I'll get the girls up."

Jonas lit the lamp in the kitchen before he put on his heavy winter coat, black hat, work shoes, and gloves. He lit another Coleman lamp to take with him and stepped out into the winter night.

Cold, but no wind, he thought. Thank goodness. He ran to the buggy shed, one side of which housed the horses. He and Sue Ann had lived in that half of the shed when they were first married seven years ago. Now they had a real house, and their former living quarters had been turned into three stalls.

The pungent aroma of horses greeted Jonas as he opened the door and hung the lantern from a hook along the wall. Lightning, Patsy, and Preacher were each in their own stall, and they watched with interest as Jonas grabbed a bridle and approached Lightning. "Hey, big guy, we're going for a quick ride up to the Jacobs," Jonas explained, slipping the bit into the large bay gelding's mouth and the headpiece over his ears. "Let's go."

Jonas turned the knob on the lantern down until the bright white light died, and left it hanging on its hook. He led Lightning out into the night, looped the reins over the horse's head and shoulders, and vaulted onto his back. Jonas touched his heels to Lightning's sides, and they were off.

Times like these, it'd sure be nice to have a telephone, not to mention a car, Jonas thought as Lightning galloped the three-fourths mile to the Jacobs. But part of being Amish meant not having those "worldly conveniences." They didn't own them so they wouldn't be subject to the influences and control that things like phones and televisions could have over their lives. But they could utilize the automobiles and telephones of "English" people.

Strangely enough, Jonas noted, the pickup he drove to work every day was sitting in their yard. But that was a work vehicle—not to be used for personal trips. Not even for the impending birth of a baby.

Jonas remembered another very cold night, way back when he was 16. New Year's Eve, it'd been. He'd gone to a party at the home of his boss, Harlan Schmidt. Harlan's daughter, Debbie, had invited him. In fact, it had been their first date—one that led to a six-month relationship with Debbie, an "English" girl. Anyway, that night—in a blizzard—his buggy had lost a wheel, and he'd ended up walking in the frigid storm, leading Lightning, hoping he wouldn't freeze before he found a farm at which to take shelter. That night he'd been scared—scared he would die. Scared God was punishing him for hanging out with the

English kids, for getting involved with Debbie. His parents had always insisted that he was meant to stay Amish, and that leaving would be disrespectful to them and against what God intended for him.

Well, he'd lived through that night, and here he was again, out in the cold with Lightning. This time it wasn't his survival that worried him, but that of his wife and unborn child. His heart suddenly raced with the fear. What if Sue Ann was having trouble? What if the baby's cord was wrapped around his neck, like had happened to some friends of theirs? What if ... oh God no ... the baby was stillborn? What if the time it was taking to get to the Jacobs and back to Sue Ann was the difference between life and death? What if...? Jonas urged Lightning to go faster, and the cold didn't seem to matter anymore.

❖ ❖ ❖

"We'll drop the girls off at Sue Ann's parents on the way into town," Jonas instructed Cindy Jacobs from the back seat of her car. Sue Ann was in the front with Cindy; Jonas had Becca and Lydianne with him.

"At least this didn't happen a week ago during that snowstorm," Cindy commented. "You guys should plan your children so they aren't born in the winter."

Jonas heard the teasing in her voice. Cindy knew that the Amish *Ordnung* didn't allow them to practice birth control. She also knew, from being in the Amish community, that the *Ordnung*—the understood behavior by which the Amish were expected to live—couldn't control what happened in the bedrooms of Amish couples.

"Seemed like good planning on this one, at the time," Jonas joked back. He and Sue Ann knew Cindy and her husband, Matt, quite well, and they were able to talk and share quite freely amongst themselves. "Am I right, Sue

Ann?" Jonas asked.

"It always seems like good planning 'at the time,'" Sue Ann responded wryly. Both Cindy and Jonas laughed.

Sue Ann let out a sharp gasp and clutched her protruding stomach. When the pain had passed, she glanced at Cindy and said, "Why don't men have to share in this part too?"

"I hear you," Cindy agreed. "It never did seem fair to me either."

❖ ❖ ❖

Enos J. Bontrager was born at 11:13 a.m. that morning in the Wellsford Medical Center. As Jonas held the wrinkled, red little miracle of love, emotions flooded his soul and spilled out through his clear blue eyes. He'd felt this with the arrival of Becca and Lydianne too—the incredible joy of holding his offspring, of seeing the perfection of the tiny human being in his arms.

But this time, there was something more. This time he was holding his son. A son to carry on his name. A son to teach about farming, and fishing, and finding his way through life. A son to be his friend.

He was named after Jonas's best friend as a teenager, Enos Miller. Fun-loving, pushing-the-edge Enos. Even though the tragedy that took Enos's life happened almost twelve years ago, Jonas could still see Enos lying on the concrete parking lot, and feel the shock of hearing the doctor say, "There was nothing we could do."

Now he held a namesake, a tiny new Enos, in his arms. As Jonas marveled at his son, he offered a prayer of thanksgiving and supplication to God. "Please protect him from harm," he prayed. "And help me to be a good father."

❖ ❖ ❖

E.J., as the Bontragers called the new addition to their

family, thrived under the love and care of his parents and sisters. Becca was old enough to help with little things that Sue Ann asked her to do, including keeping an eye on Lydianne when she was with E.J. "My baby," Lydianne called him, and they never were quite sure how she might try to play with "her baby." But she learned quickly what her limits were, and usually went back to playing with her doll, which she could handle any way she wanted to.

On a Saturday afternoon in mid-May, a van drove into the Bontrager yard. Jonas and Sue Ann had been expecting these special visitors ever since they got a letter in April saying, "We want to come visit our first great-grandson." Jacob and Fannie Bontrager were Fred's parents—Jonas's grandparents—and lived in Indiana. Although in their late 70's, they were both still active and healthy. Along with several other couples wanting to make the trip to Kansas, they'd hired a driver with a van to take them.

After the initial greetings, Sue Ann led Jacob and Fannie into the house, and Jonas stayed behind to talk to the van driver a bit.

"You're Merv Smucker, aren't you?" Jonas studied the man dressed in conservative, but not Amish, clothing.

"Yes," Merv answered. "And I remember you. I took you and a bunch of guys to a barn party in Missouri—must have been almost ten years ago."

Jonas laughed out loud with recognition. "That's right! The one where Edwin broke his ankle!"

"Yeah, you guys were swinging out of a barn on a rope, and the rope tore," Merv remembered. "I had to take Edwin to the hospital and sit there most of the night with him. What's he up to these days?"

"Oh, settled down like most of us," Jonas smiled. "Married, farming, has two kids."

"Looks like you're doing okay too," Merv noted as his

eyes took in the new white house, buggy shed, neatly kept yard, and horses grazing nearby. "Nice-looking horse you've got there. The black one."

"That's Preacher," Jonas said, then realized the name must sound strange. "The neighbor kids called him that, and I guess it stuck. He just turned a year."

"Can he run?" Merv asked, walking toward the fence to get a closer look.

"You should see him!" Jonas smiled, trying not to sound proud. "When he lets loose, its beautiful!"

"That his dam?"

"Yeah, she was bred when I bought her at a sale. I just liked the looks of the mare. She's a thoroughbred, but I figured I could breed her to a standardbred stud around here and get a good buggy horse for the future. I had no idea what I was getting as far as this colt."

Seeing and hearing the men at the fence, Preacher had come up to check it out. As a yearling, he stood as tall as his mother, and Jonas knew he wasn't through growing. He was maturing into a fine speciman of a horse, and loved people. Still too young to break to drive or ride, he didn't suspect anything other than some grain and attention when people showed up. Lightning usually played a "I don't want to go" game with Jonas when he caught him, but not Preacher. Not yet. He nuzzled Jonas's arm.

"Do you know anything about his sire?" Merv reached over and stroked the shiny black neck.

"Nope. We didn't get any papers with the mare."

"He looks an awful lot like a horse that used to race up at the track in Landers. Couple of years ago, I think. Pitch black, just like this. He won a lot of races there."

"You don't think...." Jonas turned to stare at Merv.

"I don't know. Maybe I could find out though. Do you know who sold her? Was it a stable?"

"Don't remember. I'd have to see if it said something on the bill of sale."

"If you have time, do that before I pick up Jacob and Fannie next week. If you find the name of the owner, I bet I could find out about his sire. Wouldn't it be wild if it was that race horse?"

Jonas didn't answer right away as a mixture of thoughts suddenly invaded his consciousness. If Preacher had racing blood in him, could he still be a good buggy horse? Or would he be too high-strung? He'd noticed more and more fire in Preacher as he grew older, but he'd never been mean or unmanageable. Maybe Preacher belonged on the track, in which case.... Well, Amish people didn't own race horses.

Jonas studied the tall young stallion in front of him, and finally answered Merv's question. "Yeah, I guess that'd be quite a deal."

23

Chapter
3

Chapter 4

Keepers

The letter arrived several weeks later. Sue Ann showed it to Jonas when he came home from work.

"Well, what do you know," he said, folding and slipping it back into the envelope.

"What are you going to do?" Sue Ann asked.

"I'm not sure. What do you think?"

"I don't know either. It shouldn't be such a big decision. Either they go, or they stay. Or one goes and one stays," Sue Ann said. "Becca! Come set the table for supper!"

"It's more complicated than that," Jonas said, picking up E.J. from his playpen.

"You tend to make things complicated, Jonas," Sue Ann teased. "I bet, when your mom asked you to set the table when you were a kid, you wondered if you should put on knives *and* forks *and* spoons. The green glasses or the Tupperware? Little bowls or big bowls?" Sue Ann walked to the chair where Jonas sat with E.J. and gave Jonas a light kiss on the forehead. "But you know I love you for it— that's what makes life interesting."

"Just for that, I'm not going to tell you why this deal isn't so simple," Jonas said, his mouth pursed in a fake little pout. "I'll talk to Becca about it instead."

"What, Daddy?" Becca had been listening, but obviously now the conversation called for her input.

"Well, there's a guy in Indiana who's interested in buying Preacher," Jonas said, watching his six-year-old closely for her reaction.

Becca stopped in the middle of setting a knife on the table, and instead shook it slowly at her father. The look in her dark eyes wasn't a threat—it wasn't even anger or a tantrum-in-the-making. The brown eyes—the ones she got from her mother—simply made a statement. "You can't sell Preacher, Dad," she said, and then calmly continued setting the table.

Jonas and Sue Ann exchanged glances. Jonas didn't take any sassing back from his children, and the waving knife had caught him off guard. But he knew it had simply been Becca's exclamation point—one she happened to have in her hand.

"And why can't I sell Preacher?" Jonas pushed the issue.

"Because he's ours. We all like him. Ben and Marie love him. And you do too, Daddy," Becca stated.

"Well, how about if we let Merv—that's the guy in Indiana—borrow Preacher for a little while? He says he could break him to ride. Then when Preacher comes back, you could ride him."

Becca was quiet, and Jonas could almost see the wheels spinning in her brain. She absentmindedly flicked back the white strings hanging down from her covering and seemed to be concentrating on the glasses she was putting on the table.

"Could we go see him?" she finally asked.

"Probably not. Indiana's too far away."

"How long would he be there?"

"I don't know."

"Well, then," she paused, her hands on her young hips, "I don't like the sound of it at all."

Jonas smiled at her grown-up response—she'd obviously seen someone else do that. But he struggled inside, knowing this wasn't going to be an easy decision.

❖ ❖ ❖

Jonas felt like he needed to talk to someone else—someone who appreciated a good horse but could also help him see clearly through his decisions. He and Sue Ann decided to go to his parents after supper. Jonas hitched Lightning up to the hack buggy while Sue Ann collected the children, washed off the worst of the day's grime from their faces, and changed Lydianne's dress. Becca had stayed fairly clean that day, but the three-year-old was another story.

Esther greeted her grandchildren with open arms and cookies, and while she took Sue Ann to look at her garden, Jonas found Fred working on the drill. A rain the day before was keeping farmers out of the fields, but as soon as they could, they'd be in there planting milo. Wheat harvest would follow soon. All of that depending on the weather, of course.

"Got a letter from Merv Smucker today," Jonas said to Fred, who was sitting cross-legged on the ground, replacing a part on the drill. "He found out that Preacher's sire used to be a race horse out there in Indiana. A big black stallion named Legacy."

"Oh?" Fred looked up at his son. "And?"

"And he wants to buy Preacher, or at least take him back there to break him. He went to the stable that owns the stallion and he wants to take Patsy back to that stud to breed her and see if she'll have another colt like Preacher."

"Why's Merv so interested in Preacher and Patsy?"

"He saw him when he stopped at our place last month. And now that he knows who the sire is … well, I think Merv's hoping to get a race horse out of the deal."

"What are you going to do?"

"I don't know. What would you do?"

Fred grunted as he tightened a nut on the drill. "Put a pretty price on 'em. If Merv's willing to pay it, sell 'em."

"I'm not sure Merv will pay a lot, and I'm not sure I want to sell them. Especially Preacher. The kids are really attached to him."

"The kids?" Fred laughed. "But not you?"

"Yeah, I like him. I think he could become a good buggy horse. Lightning's getting older, and I need to be thinking about a replacement sometime down the road."

"He's a thoroughbred, Jonas. They don't make buggy horses. They don't pace, and they're high-strung. Best thing you can hope for out of him is a fast riding horse."

"Maybe you're right. But ... I'd still like to try."

"How old is he?" Fred asked.

"A year."

"It's time you get him cut."

"I know."

"Well, it's up to you, what you do. Me, I like horses, but they have to earn their keep." Fred stood up and wiped the back of his greasy hand across his forehead. "Let's go in and have some tea. And I need to see those grandkids of mine."

Later that night, after the girls were in bed, Jonas and Sue Ann sat in the dark on the front porch. Sue Ann was nursing and rocking E.J. to sleep, and Jonas sat in the porch swing he'd made for Sue Ann for their fifth anniversary.

"I'm sorry if I hurt your feelings when I said you make everything complicated," Sue Ann said quietly from the rocking chair. "I know this horse thing is a big deal for you. Did you get any advice from your dad?"

"You didn't hurt my feelings," Jonas responded. "I know I do that. Dad had a simple answer—put a high price on the horses and sell them if Merv's willing to pay."

"But that isn't a good solution," Sue Ann's voice reflected a statement rather than a question. She knew Jonas well.

"If we sell Preacher, we have to start all over with a colt," Jonas said. "He's a good horse. Why should I sell him? And Patsy, she's a good brood mare. We'll want more colts in the future. Why sell her?"

"Then keep them."

"I will," Jonas said firmly. "But I think I'll send them to Indiana. Can't hurt to breed Patsy to the same stallion—we can always sell that colt. And if Merv wants to break Preacher for us, that's fine. We'll get him back, and hopefully we'll have a great riding and driving horse."

Chapter 4

"Have fun telling the kids."

"I've thought about that. I think we should get them a pony they can ride. It'll help take their minds off Preacher, and give them something more their size to learn on. Marie and Ben and Becca are just the right ages to start with a Shetland pony."

❖ ❖ ❖

Jonas left by 5:00 a.m. the next morning, like he always did, to go to work at the Schmidt dairy. He'd been employed there for 12 years—ever since he turned 16. Working for the Schmidts had its perks. For one thing, Jonas really enjoyed his job, and Harlan had put him in charge of the whole dairy herd. Being able to drive their pickup to and from work was another advantage. And having access to a phone came in real handy sometimes.

Like this morning. As soon as the milking was done, Jonas used his credit card to call Merv in Indiana. He told Merv he wasn't ready to sell either of the horses, but he'd be willing to let Merv borrow Preacher until he was well broke, and he could also take Patsy back to be bred to Legacy. Merv said he'd leave later that day and be at Jonas's place the next morning.

The next morning, a Saturday, was Jonas's weekend off,

so he didn't have to worry about missing work to meet Merv. He was concerned about one thing, though, and that was loading Preacher in a horse trailer. He'd never been in a trailer before, and Jonas knew from experience how difficult it could be to get a horse in a trailer for the first time. The only factor that might help a little bit was that Patsy would be in there too.

Chapter 4

Jonas had explained to Becca at the breakfast table that he'd decided to let Preacher go to Indiana, but that he wasn't selling him. He'd also promised her a Shetland pony "real soon" that she could ride, and she seemed appeased. She insisted on watching them load the horses, however, and saying good-bye to Preacher.

Jonas caught Patsy, attached a lead rope to her halter, and led her into the trailer with barely a change in her stride. She'd done this many times before.

Preacher followed Jonas dutifully until Jonas stepped into the trailer and expected Preacher to go in as well. He'd never seen anything like that contraption before, much less been asked to go into it. No way. Huh-uh. He tried to back up while Jonas, equally determined, held on tightly to the lead rope. Jonas quickly looped the rope around part of the trailer for leverage and to help him hold the strong yearling. Preacher's neck was stretched tight, his halter and rope taut. His agonized breathing came in shallow gasps, and his eyes rolled back in fear.

"Daddy!" Becca cried from where she stood, watching. "You're hurting Preacher!"

"Stay back, Becca!" Jonas ordered from inside the trailer. "Maybe you should go back to the house."

Becca didn't leave, but neither did she say anything more. She knew she'd better keep quiet if she wanted to stay and watch. And she did, as much as it hurt to see what was happening.

"Come on, Preacher, it's okay," Jonas encouraged. "Come on, big guy. Patsy's in here. You can do it."

Preacher leaned forward just enough to ease the tension on his halter. He stood at the trailer entrance, breathing hard, regarding Jonas.

"Here's some grain, Preacher. Come on," Jonas continued in a low soothing voice. He shook a can of grain just out of Preacher's reach.

Chapter
4

Preacher knew grain, and he loved it. He stretched his neck into the trailer, his lips begging for the treat. But his feet remained firmly on the ground.

"Merv!" Jonas called. "Come try lifting his front feet in."

Under normal conditions, Jonas could do anything with Preacher's feet. He'd been lifting them since the day he was born. But these weren't normal conditions, at least not as far as Preacher was concerned.

Merv slipped beside Preacher, keeping an eye on the horse's ears and body language. A horse in this position could throw himself down, lash out with his feet, kick—anything. A person couldn't be too careful.

"Let's go, Preacher," Merv said, reaching down to pick up the right front leg standing in front of the trailer. He lifted it the 12 inches up to the trailer floor and set it down.

Now Preacher felt very unbalanced, and he didn't like it. Just as he started to pull back again, Jonas tightened the rope a little more. Once again, Preacher pulled back with 800 pounds of determination. Suddenly, without warning, the rope shredded, and Preacher crashed on his back legs with a thud. He recovered in an instant and whirled around, wild-eyed and ready to run.

Jonas was out of the trailer in a second—talking, calling, assuring the frightened horse. He worked his way up to Preacher and reached for his halter.

"Get two more lead ropes out of the shed," he told

Merv. "Strong ones!"

Jonas hooked one of the ropes to Preacher's halter again, the other one he tied to the end gate of the trailer.

"We'll encourage him from the back," he said, and Merv nodded knowingly. He'd been through this before too.

Chapter 4

It took a lot of time and patience to get Preacher to the position he'd been in before the rope tore, but finally he was standing with one front foot in the trailer. Merv slipped around to the other side. Leaning heavily on the horse, he lifted the other unwilling foot up, then backed away quickly and grabbed the rope tied to the end gate. He slowly pulled the gate toward him until it bumped Preacher's hindquarters. Preacher jumped. Jonas pulled quickly. Merv pulled the gate closer. With one lunge, Preacher stood in the trailer, trembling. Merv latched the door while Jonas quickly tied Preacher, then he escaped through a small side door.

Jonas wiped the sweat from his brow and grinned at Merv. "Maybe part of his training at your place can include trailer loading."

"Yeah, there'll be an extra charge for that," he chuckled. "But we sure can do it."

"Speaking of extra charges, I was wondering if you'd want to get a vet out and have him gelded while he's there," Jonas said. "I was going to do that this summer, and I don't really want to wait till he gets back."

"Sure you don't want to keep him a stallion?" Merv wondered.

"I don't know why. I don't need a stallion. And I sure don't need a horse acting studly around here—they're too dangerous."

"Okay, we'll see what we can do," Merv answered. He didn't sound very convinced, Jonas thought. But maybe it was just his imagination.

"I'll bring Patsy back when we know she's bred," Merv said. "I'd better hit the road now. We've got a long trip ahead of us."

Becca walked slowly up to the trailer and stared at what she could see of Preacher's head. She waved slowly. "Bye, Preacher. When you come back, I'm going to ride you."

33

Chapter
4

Chapter 5

Legacy

The trip to Indiana that Thanksgiving was either a great idea or they were crazy, Jonas thought before they left. They'd never traveled that far with their young family. At almost ten months, E.J. was one active little boy, and certainly not inclined to spend hours upon hours in a car seat. But Fred and Esther had decided to go visit Fred's parents, and virtually begged Jonas and Sue Ann to go along. "They should see the children," Esther kept saying.

When Becca had heard they were going to Indiana, she hadn't hesitated a moment before declaring, "Then we can go see Preacher!"

The 16-hour drive went better than Jonas and Sue Ann expected. They'd deliberately decided to drive during the night, in hopes that the children would sleep away a lot of the hours, and that had worked for the most part. Everyone was ready to escape the close quarters by the time they arrived at Jacob and Fannie's on Thursday morning.

Merv came to pick up Jonas and Becca on Saturday morning to go see Preacher. Jonas was looking forward to the excursion with his daughter, and he was eager to see Preacher again. Merv's occasional letters over the past five months had filled him in briefly, but it was sort of a case of "out of sight, out of mind." Life had gone on without Preacher around, but now it'd sure be fun to see him again.

Merv turned down a long lane bordered with white horse fences—the kind Jonas had seen in pictures of Kentucky. Even in the gray coldness of the Indiana countryside, Jonas could see the beauty of this horse farm. A stone sign at the entry said "Springdale Stables." Jonas recognized it as the name of the place that had sold Patsy, and the home of Preacher's sire, Legacy.

Chapter 5

"I want to show you something here first," Merv said by way of explanation. Jonas knew Merv could feel the unspoken question. This wasn't Merv's farm. This wasn't where Jonas thought Preacher was staying.

Merv stopped his van in front of a long white building, perfectly trimmed in dark green. Immaculate white fences connected it to other matching buildings, and Jonas could only think that this was horse heaven. For horses, and for people who loved them.

Jonas took Becca's hand as they stepped out into the biting north wind and followed Merv toward the building. Inside, the first thing Jonas noticed was the temperature. Warm. Comfortable. At the same time, his eyes took in the rows of green-trimmed, white stalls hugging either side of the building. In the middle, a large arena awaited the next workout session. In fact, as they stood there, a gate on the far end of the building opened and a horse entered the arena, tossing its head impatiently. The small man on the thousand pounds of pent-up energy rode as if he could do it in his sleep.

Jonas and Becca followed Merv down the right side, stopping occasionally to admire a horse in one of the stalls. When they reached the far corner, they came to an enclosure twice the size of the other stalls. Large dark-green letters over the door proclaimed "LEGACY."

Merv strode up to the door, almost like a proud father in a nursery window. Only this wasn't the baby. This was the father—the winning stallion, the stud responsible for Preacher. "Check this out," Merv said.

Jonas peered into the spacious, well-lit, square room. He felt a rush growing inside of him, working its way through his soul, shining from his eyes, spreading his face in an uncontrollable smile of pleasure. The magnificent black stallion in front of him was Preacher, only much more so. Taller, stronger, full of life and virility. The bright eyes regarded him with intelligence and interest. Jonas couldn't take his eyes off the horse. He'd never seen anything like this before. Perfectly groomed, the horse was the picture of power and speed—the legacy of excellent breeding. No wonder he'd won so many races.

Becca's voice finally broke through the spell. "Daddy! I can't see! Hold me up!"

Jonas lifted Becca up to see over the half-door. "Is that Preacher?" she asked.

"No," Jonas answered. "But it could be someday. It could be."

"Wow," Becca said, almost reverently.

"Now let's go see Preacher," Merv said, and began to walk across the large shed to the other side.

"He's not here, is he?" Jonas asked. "Isn't he at your place?"

"Well, actually, he *is* here," Merv admitted. "I talked to the manager, and he's letting me board him here. The training facilities are so much nicer, especially now in the winter."

The trio reached the long line of stalls on the opposite side of the building. Merv walked up to the door of the second one from the end and opened it.

"Hey, Preacher-man, you've got company," he spoke to the large black horse munching on a slab of alfalfa. "You remember these folks?"

Jonas and Becca stood in the open doorway. Preacher

36

Chapter
5

eyed them with interest. By the time Becca's soft voice had uttered the words, "Come 'ere, Preacher," he'd already taken a step in their direction. In a moment, his lips were nuzzling Jonas's hand.

"He's so tall, Daddy!" Becca said, reaching up to stroke the gleaming black neck. "And he still has the white hair on his chest."

"He's quite a horse," Merv said. "Let's take him out where you can see him better."

Merv led Preacher out of his stall and into the arena, with Jonas and Becca following. Jonas was amazed at the muscle tone Preacher had added since he'd been gone. Obviously, someone was working with him and building his body into fine form.

"Looks to me like you've been spending a lot of time training him," Jonas commented.

"Well, I've had a little help," Merv said. "One of the trainers here has taken an interest in bringing him along. What do you think?"

Jonas let his eyes feast on the beautiful horse standing with alert confidence at Merv's side. Without a doubt, Legacy's blood flowed through Preacher like water rushing down a dam. Harnessed power. It shone through his eyes and rippled under his skin.

"I think he looks good," Jonas answered. "Very good." He paused and studied the horse closer. "I think it looks like you haven't gelded him."

"That's one of the things we need to talk about," Merv said. "Let's walk him around the arena, and we'll talk. Becca, would you like to ride him?"

Becca's dark eyes widened with surprise. "You mean I can? Now?"

"I don't see why not," Merv answered. "Jonas, just lift her on."

Jonas lifted his six-year-old daughter onto Preacher's back. The horse side-stepped a bit, then turned his head to see what was going on.

"Whoa, Preacher, it's okay," Merv assured. "It's just Becca. She's lighter than Lisa."

"Lisa?" Jonas wondered.

"Lisa's a young jockey that's started riding Preacher. See, Jonas," Merv started walking slowly, leading Preacher. "The stable here has taken an interest in Preacher. They think he has potential. They want to race him next summer as a two-year-old."

Jonas let the words sink in. Even then, he knew he'd need a lot more time to process what he'd just heard.

"So, that's why you didn't geld him," Jonas finally spoke.

"Right. It'd affect his development. Plus, if he ends up being a winner, you may want to use him as a sire."

"Daddy!" Becca called from Preacher's back. "I'm riding Preacher! Can we take him home now?"

"Not yet, Honey," Jonas said.

"But why not? You said he's coming here to get broke, and then he'd come home and we could ride him. He's broke now, isn't he?"

"Yes, he is. We'll talk about it later, Becca. Just enjoy your ride for now."

❖ ❖ ❖

"Well, did you have fun? How was Preacher?" Sue Ann greeted Jonas and Becca from her position at the kitchen counter when they returned to Jacob and Fannie's house around noon. Sue Ann was mashing potatoes by hand while E.J. crawled around on the floor at her feet. He tilted his head up at his father and big sister and drooled a grin.

"I rode Preacher!" Becca exclaimed. "Where's Lydianne? I've gotta tell her!" She scampered into the living room.

"Lydianne! Guess what I did!"

"She *rode* Preacher?" Sue Ann questioned Jonas, who'd bent down to pick up E.J.

"Yep, she did," he said, noncommittaly. "They've been working with him. Got him broke. He looks good. And what did my little man do while I was gone?" he asked, holding E.J. up in the air. E.J. giggled and Jonas put him on his shoulders for a piggy-back ride. "You want to go for a ride too? Let's go find your sisters!"

The topic of Preacher came up again over lunch when Fred asked Jonas how he was doing. Jonas tried to appease his father's curiosity without spilling his conversation with Merv to everyone gathered at the table. It was more than they needed to know at this point.

Later that evening when Jonas and Sue Ann were getting ready for bed by lamp light, Sue Ann broached the issue.

"What happened this morning, Jonas?"

"What do you mean?"

"I mean you haven't wanted to say much about your time with Preacher. What's going on?"

Relieved to be able to talk about it in private, Jonas told Sue Ann about Preacher. How not just Merv but a trainer and jockey at the stable had been working with him. How they wanted to put Preacher on the track next spring.

"I don't know what to do," he concluded. "I need to let Merv know before we go back," Jonas crawled into bed beside Sue Ann and turned down the lamp on the bedside table.

"What happens if you let him race?" Sue Ann's voice came softly from close to Jonas's ear.

"He could get it in his blood and never settle down when we bring him home. Then we have no use for him."

"Can we even own him if we let Preacher race? The

church won't allow it!"

"You're probably right," Jonas conceded.

"What happens if you bring him home now?" Sue Ann wondered.

Chapter
5

"He's still not broke to drive. We'd have to get somebody to do that. Then, hopefully we could start using him. Man, he'd look good pulling a buggy!" Jonas smiled in the dark.

"How did he act when Becca was riding him? She wasn't riding him by herself, was she?"

"No, no, Merv was leading him. And Preacher was real calm."

"But he's a thoroughbred. I'm a little bit worried about that with the kids around here. If you bring him home, Becca will want to ride him."

"I know. She really loves that horse."

Sue Ann sighed deeply beside Jonas. "Honey, maybe it'd just be better to sell him."

Jonas frowned in the darkness. No. He did not want to sell Preacher.

"I know," Sue Ann murmured sleepily. "You don't want to. Good-night, Honey."

"Good-night," Jonas kissed Sue Ann's dark hair. Then he lay awake, long after he felt her fall asleep beside him.

Chapter 6

Mose

Little E.J. was going to be a year old a few days before his great-grandfather Moses Eash had his birthday, so the family planned a big party for the two of them. It'd be held at the home of Cris and Rachel Eash, Sue Ann's parents. That way, Mose, who lived in a "Dawdi house" (Grandpa house) next door, wouldn't have to go out if the weather turned nasty.

Mose was past 80 now, and he'd lost his wife to cancer a year ago. Since then, his age seemed to be really taking a toll on him. Everyone knew they had to TALK REAL LOUD when addressing Mose if they wanted him to hear them, and a cataract on one of his eyes had affected his vision considerably. Arthritis had set into his hips, and he moved slowly with the aid of a cane.

Mose still insisted on driving his own horse and buggy, and the family lived in fear of him having an accident. But, unlike people with a driver's license who could get it revoked if they didn't pass the test, Mose didn't need a license to drive his buggy. He just hitched up his trusty old horse and headed down the road.

While Mose's body seemed to be wearing out, and his energy for life decreasing, his mind remained brilliant and sharp. He still preached in church, although he usually allowed himself the luxury of sitting down for the last part of his sermon. He knew the Bible and he understood the *Ordnung* better than anyone. As bishop, that was his job. Age and experience had earned him a position of status and respect in his community.

Chapter 6

The evening of the birthday party, Mose sat in the rocking chair in the corner of the living room. The men were gathered on chairs and couches in the same room, catching up on the latest news and gossip. The women inhabited the kitchen area, and the half-dozen great-grandchildren played wherever they chose. At one point, E.J. toddled his way over to Mose and stood in front of the old man, offering him a ragged teddy bear. Mose gratefully took the bear, then reached out his arms to the boy.

"Come here, E.J.," he said. "Come sit with me."

But E.J. wasn't in a sitting mood. Having found a babysitter for his bear, he wandered off to other important people and places.

The evening passed quickly, and soon husbands were telling wives to get the kids dressed while they went out to get the buggy. Jonas was almost out the door when he heard someone calling his name. He turned to see Mose beckoning him over to his rocker.

"If you could wait a minute, I'd be much obliged," Mose said without explanation. "Until the others are gone, if you don't mind."

Jonas said "sure," and went to tell Sue Ann.

Sensing that Mose might want to speak to Jonas alone, Sue Ann and her parents made themselves scarce as soon as everyone else had left. The fact that Jonas would have to talk loudly for Mose's sake meant they'd probably hear half of the conversation anyway. Jonas sat down on the couch close to Mose's rocker and waited.

"Whatever happened to that black horse of yours?" Mose asked.

Jonas's heart skipped a beat. This wasn't just small talk. Mose had a reason to be asking about Preacher.

"He's up in Indiana. Getting trained."

"It's a long way to go to have a buggy horse trained," the old man probed gently but insistently.

Chapter 6

"Yeah, I know. Guy named Merv Smucker up there wanted to work with him." Jonas had the feeling he was telling Mose things that Mose already knew.

"I hear tell they're gonna race him this summer," Mose said.

"Well, they're talking about it, yes." Jonas braced himself for the reply.

"You told them they could do that?" Mose's voice remained calm and quiet.

"I told Merv if they put the horse on the track, I didn't want my name included and I didn't want any money he might win. As long as he's up there, he's basically their horse."

"So why don't you sell him?"

Jonas leaned forward on the couch and studied his clasped hands. The ticking of the clock in the room seemed to count his discomfort.

"I guess because he's a good horse. I like him. I have hopes of him coming back and settling down into a buggy horse."

"Jonas, I appreciate a good horse. We all do," it was Mose's turn to lean forward slowly, methodically. "But the other ministers and I felt it was time to speak to you. We're concerned about you having a race horse. Our *Ordnung* won't allow that," Mose paused as he stroked his long white beard. "I'll tell them what you told me. We'll see."

Mose reached down to the floor and picked up his cane. "Time for this old man to go to bed," he closed the conversation, slowly standing up. "Good-night."

"Good-night," Jonas replied.

❖ ❖ ❖

Jonas got nervous every time he talked to Mose or any of the other ministers in the course of their business, social, and church contacts in the weeks that followed. But no one said anything more about Preacher, and Jonas wondered if he had been warned and that was the end of it. He certainly hoped so.

Chapter
6

Merv didn't write Jonas at all that winter, and Jonas was almost relieved. Although he was curious about Preacher's training, he didn't really want to know how he was coming along. If he didn't know, maybe no one else would, he rationalized. But he knew the racing season began in April, and he wondered if and when Preacher would be running.

Late in May, Patsy gave birth to another black foal—a filly this time. Jonas and Sue Ann didn't see the arrival of Preacher's full-blooded sister—she was standing shyly next to her mother when Jonas went out that morning to feed the horses. Although the newborn had her sire's black coat, she also sported four white socks—a gift from her dam. Jonas looked for the small patch of white hair on her chest, but it wasn't there.

Becca and Lydianne, as well as the neighbor kids, Ben and Marie, were all thrilled to have another colt. They immediately began begging Jonas and Sue Ann to take them in to see the baby, and they talked about what to name it.

One afternoon, when the filly was about a week old, Mose's old horse turned slowly into the Bontrager lane. Sue Ann looked up from the garden she was weeding when she heard the trudging of the horse and the rolling buggy wheels in the sandy driveway. She was pleasantly surprised to see who it was. Mose didn't come visit that often.

The old man slowly stepped down from his buggy and tied his horse up at the hitching post. Sue Ann met him there.

"Hi, Dawdi! It's good to see you!" she greeted. "Sorry I look such a mess!"

"Ach, you look fine," Mose returned. "Anybody who's been working in God's good earth always looks fine to me."

"You want to come in?" Sue Ann invited.

Before she could answer, Becca and Lydianne ran up to Mose and Sue Ann. They'd been making mud pies, and Mose chuckled loudly at their mud-splattered faces, arms, hands, and dresses. "Looks like these two have been working in God's good earth too!"

"Come see our new huchley," Lydianne took Mose's hand in her grimy little one. Becca grabbed his other wrinkled white hand and they led him to the corral.

Sue Ann went into the house to get a drink. She'd just stepped outside again when she heard the terrified cries of her girls. She ran to meet them coming away from the horse corral.

"Mommy! Mommy! It's Dawdi! Something's wrong!" Becca screamed.

Sue Ann flew to where Mose lay crumpled on the ground, just inside the fence. "Dawdi! Dawdi!" she called, kneeling beside him. He was mumbling something she couldn't understand, and a cut on his head dripped blood onto her hands.

Several hours later, in the waiting room of Wellsford Medical Center, Sue Ann told the gathered family members what happened after she discovered Dawdi. "I had to get him out of there," she wept. "I didn't know if one of the horses had kicked him or what. He was talking but not making any sense, and I don't think he could understand me. I had to pull him through the gate."

Jonas held Sue Ann's hand and tried to comfort her.

"And then I had to go to the Jacobs to call for help," Sue Ann recounted. "It seemed to take forever to catch Lightning, hitch him up, and then get the kids into the buggy. I hated to leave him there, but what could I do?"

"You did everything you could," Sue Ann's mother, Rachel, assured.

"I called 911, and then hurried back. The ambulance came, finally, and brought him here," Sue Ann sobbed quietly.

A doctor in scrubs entered the waiting room, and everyone's eyes turned toward him. "Is this the family of Mr. Eash?" he asked. They nodded, and Jonas squeezed Sue Ann's hand tighter.

"It appears Mr. Eash had a stroke," the doctor said. "A severe stroke. His vital signs are stable, but he's unconscious. That's about all I can tell you right now."

"You're certain it was a stroke?" Jonas questioned. "It wasn't a blow to the head, like a kick from a horse?"

"He does have a good-sized cut on his head, but we think it was from his fall, from hitting the fence," the doctor said. "It seems to me a horse kick would have done more damage."

Maybe not if it's a week-old colt, Jonas thought to himself. He looked at Sue Ann, and read the same thing in her eyes.

❖ ❖ ❖

News of Mose's accident traveled fast in the Amish community, and so did the speculation. The fact that nobody knew for certain if he'd been kicked by Jonas's new colt added fuel to the gossip. Becca and Lydianne had left Mose at the gate while they ran to the shed to get the little blue halter. According to Becca, Mose had said he'd help them put it on. When the girls returned moments later, Mose was on the ground. Patsy and her filly were nearby.

On the one hand, Mose couldn't hear or see very well, so he had no business messing with that colt, some people said. On the other hand, wasn't that filly out of some high-powered stallion in Indiana? Jonas had just been asking for trouble, breeding his mare to that stallion. What was he thinking anyway? And so the rumor mill worked its way through the Amish homes, places of business, and church.

Mose lay unconscious for a week, and when he finally opened his eyes, they stared vacantly at the hospital ceiling. No amount of talking into his ear or family faces leaning over him brought a trace of recognition to his eyes. Machines kept his body alive, but family members felt his soul yearned to go, to be released from its earthly constraints.

One evening, about a month after the accident, Jonas and Sue Ann were visiting Mose, along with Sue Ann's parents, Cris and Rachel. They'd been taking turns reading from the Bible to Mose, because they knew if he could hear anything at all, he would draw comfort from the words he knew so well. Jonas was reading from Psalm 23.

"Yea, though I walk through the valley of the shadow of death, thou art with me. Thy rod and thy staff, they comfort me," Jonas read.

Suddenly, a small cry came from Mose. Jonas stopped reading, and the family reached in to touch the frail body. For the first time since the accident, Mose's eyes seemed clear. "It's so pretty!" he said in his native Pennsylvania Dutch. "So very, very pretty!"

"What do you see, Dad?" Cris asked, gripping his father's hand.

A smile flickered across Mose's face. His eyes closed. His breathing became shallow, his breaths farther and farther apart—until there were no more.

Lightning

Jonas was worried about Sue Ann during the week following Mose's death. Her grief was more than sadness over the loss of a grandfather. She felt guilty. Responsible. She'd told Jonas more than once that she should have been able to do more. Watch Mose and the kids when they went to see the colt. Get help faster. Something.

Jonas tried to reassure her that the doctor said Mose suffered a stroke, not a kick from a horse. Sue Ann seemed to understand the words with her mind, but her emotions didn't follow. She wanted to sell the filly. She said it would always remind her of what happened to Mose.

He didn't really want to give up the filly, but Jonas agreed to sell her when she was weaning age. If it was that important to Sue Ann, he'd do it.

The death of Mose left a hole not only in the hearts of his family but also in the life of his church. The congregation would need to "make bishop" before too long. The thought of it was never far from the minds of the ministers and their wives.

Since Mose had been bishop for so long, Jonas had never seen the church make bishop. But he'd witnessed the choosing of a minister, and it was an unforgetable experience.

Four men had been nominated by the congregation to be in The Lot. Four songbooks sat stacked on a table. One of them contained a piece of paper with a Bible verse on it.

Jonas remembered the tension in the room, the breaths being held, as one by one each man took a book. And he would never forget the gasp of Samuel Wagler as he opened his book. He had physically crumpled onto a chair, as if the weight of the world had suddenly hit him squarely between the shoulder blades. And, in a sense, it had. In one quick moment, he'd gone from attending a church as a listener to leading the church and presenting sermons. The sobs of Samuel's wife and other sympathizers in the congregation had struck a deep chord in Jonas. He understood sorrow due to a death. But this was another kind of anguish. He didn't understand it, but he knew how it sounded.

Jonas wondered how it would feel to be part of a congregation as they looked to The Lot to choose their bishop. He would find out the first Sunday in October.

❖ ❖ ❖

The letter from Merv came on August 13. Jonas remembered, because it was a Friday, the 13th. He was sitting at the kitchen table, drinking a large glass of lemonade and going through the mail after he got home from the Schmidt dairy. Sue Ann was making supper, and the children were outside playing in their sandpile.

"What's this all about?" he wondered out loud, unfolding the letter and noticing two tickets enclosed in the sheet of paper. Curious, Sue Ann came to look. Jonas handed her the tickets while he read the letter.

> *Dear Jonas,* he read out loud.
> *Sorry I haven't been in touch with you more, but it's been a busy summer. A lot of Amish taking vacations, going to funerals and weddings, etc.*
> *Preacher's been in five races so far this summer,*

and he's improving with each one. He hasn't won any yet, but he's placed several times, and the trainer at the stable doesn't think he's reached his peak yet.

I know you don't want any of his winnings, so I bought a couple of train tickets with money he's won. I was hoping you and Sue Ann might want to take a short vacation up here to see relatives. It just so happens Preacher will be running at a track about three hours from here on the first Saturday in September. Your tickets would have you up here during that time, just in case you want to go see him race. I'd be glad to pick you up at the train depot and also take you to the race.

How's the filly doing? I heard a lot about her at the time when Moses Eash had his stroke or got kicked or whatever. Driving Amish around keeps me posted on a lot of the latest news, you know.

Well, gotta go. Let me know if I should pick you up at the train station.

Merv

51

Chapter
7

Jonas put the letter down on the table and took a long drink.

"Leaving Vicksburg at 5:00 a.m. on Wednesday and coming back on Tuesday," Sue Ann read from the tickets. "Almost a week. What do you think?"

"I haven't had time to think," Jonas answered. "What about the children?"

"We could probably buy tickets and take them," Sue Ann said. "Or leave them here with grandparents," she paused. "But I can't imagine a week without the children."

"Neither can I," Jonas agreed, and then a teasing smile began to build in his eyes and spread to his face. "But we might be able to live through it. We might even have fun!" He reached out to pinch her, but all he caught was a skirt as Sue Ann twisted away. "What do you think?" Jonas pulled Sue Ann into his lap. "Shall we go? Just the two of us?"

Sue Ann's dark eyes laughed back at his—the way they had so often when they were dating. Back then, Jonas was convinced he was dating the most beautiful girl among the Amish young folks. Now, after being married for eight years, he knew how she looked in the morning, before she tucked her hair under her everyday covering. He knew how she looked on Saturday night, when the covering came off and she washed the long dark hair that reached below her waist. He knew her dirt-smudged and sweaty from working in the garden, and he knew her when she stepped out of the shower. He knew her in the privacy of their bedroom. And yes, his love for the beautiful girl he'd dated had become deeper with each passing season. The death of Mose had left a shadow in her eyes that had only recently begun to lift. Maybe some time away without the children was just what they needed.

"I'll need some extra attention, since I'll be missing the children," Sue Ann was saying as she began stroking Jonas's light blond beard.

"And you shall have it. Guaranteed," Jonas kissed her lightly, then again with growing passion. "It's a deal. We'll go!"

❖ ❖ ❖

The next morning, Saturday, Sue Ann and Jonas ate an early breakfast alone. The children were still sleeping, and Jonas had to go to work.

"I'm thinking about going to Wellsford today to get some material for a dress," Sue Ann said. "I could use a new dress, and this trip gives me just the excuse I need to make one."

"Do I get a new shirt too?" Jonas wondered out loud,

tipping his cereal bowl into his mouth to drink the last of the milk.

"Yeah, and maybe I'll make you a bib to match," Sue Ann laughed. "How am I supposed to teach the children manners when they see their daddy do that?"

"They didn't see me," Jonas smiled mischievously.

"Somehow, I don't think it would have made any difference if they were sitting here," Sue Ann feigned disgust.

"Well, just for that, I'm going to have to leave," Jonas stood up from the table. "We've got a big day at the Schmidts today, and the milk inspector is coming too. I'm not sure when I'll be home." He reached over and gave Sue Ann a peck on the mouth. "Be careful going to Wellsford."

"I will."

Moments later, Jonas roared off the yard in the Schmidt pickup.

❖ ❖ ❖

As herdsman of the Schmidt dairy, it was Jonas's responsibility to manage the hired hands that came in to help with the milking, to oversee the ordering and processing of the feed for 125 cows, and to maintain the health of the herd. When he'd started working there a dozen years ago, Harlan had promised him a "calf bonus" as part of his wages. That bonus had built up into a nice little group of ten cows.

Jonas had intended to move the cows to his farm when he could afford to build a milk barn and the other facilities he'd need, but when Harlan invited him to leave the cows with his herd, it didn't take much arm-twisting for Jonas to agree. It was certainly easier to include his cows in the larger herd than to build the pens and barns at his place, and he enjoyed working with Harlan. It also gave him more flexibility than if he'd been milking his cows by himself. Like now, when he wanted to take off to go to Indiana. Jonas mentioned it to Harlan that noon as they ate lunch together in the farmhouse.

"We've got a chance to go to Indiana the first weekend in September," Jonas said, adding a large juicy tomato slice to his hamburger which was already piled high with onion, a hefty slab of cheese, homemade pickles, ketchup, and mustard. "Actually, it's from Wednesday to Tuesday. Think it'd be okay if I took off?"

Harlan had just taken a bite from his equally stacked hamburger, and it took awhile before he could answer. "Don't see why not, if you've got the help lined up for the milking."

"I'll talk to the guys," Jonas said. The words were barely out of his mouth when a loud crash of thunder split the quiet August air. Both men nearly jumped at the unexpected noise.

"I didn't even notice it getting cloudy," Jonas remarked, standing up and walking toward the window. "Must have moved in fast."

"I don't think there's rain in the forecast," Harlan added. "But you know Kansas. If you don't like the weather, wait an hour and it'll change."

The lights blinked off, then on, then off again, and another clap of thunder smashed against the house. Jonas stood at the window and watched as what appeared to be a wall of rain threw a dark, blue blanket across the western sky. Long blue streaks stretched from the horizon to the top of the cloud.

"We're in for a downpour," he said. "I just hope Sue Ann isn't on her way to or from Wellsford right about now."

"Who knows, this might not even hit on the other side of town," Harlan said, walking to the door to look out.

"I'm going to find out," Jonas said. "I'm sure she took

the open buggy to town, and it'd be bad news for them to get caught in a rainstorm." With that, he was gone, sprinting toward the pickup.

He didn't worry about Sue Ann driving the horse and buggy under normal conditions, Jonas thought as he left the Schmidt yard. Lightning was an older, dependable horse, and like all other Amish women, Sue Ann knew how to drive a horse and buggy. She'd been doing it since she was a teenager, even as her English counterparts were learning to drive a car. Sue Ann could handle a horse fine. What worried him was the fact that she and the children were out in the open without any protection from the storm. And, if for some reason, Lightning did panic …

Chapter
7

Jonas tried not to think about it as he flew through Wellsford and hoped the town cop wasn't around. He was almost out of town when the storm hit with a blast. As if he'd suddenly entered a high-powered car wash, Jonas's pickup was deluged with torrents of rain. Even with the aid of the windshield wipers, he could hardly see the road.

It seemed to take forever, but finally the first mile was behind him. He hadn't seen anyone yet. His family was probably at home, safe and sound, watching the storm through the windows.

Then, as he approached the Amish farm about a half mile from his, he noticed a dark shape in the ditch. Was it a horse and buggy? Yes! Lightning was standing among the hedge trees, tied to the fence next to the small white wooden "Amish phone booth." Sue Ann and the kids had taken refuge in there! Thank goodness!

Jonas stopped the pickup along the side of the road. As much as he wanted to see that his family was okay, there was no point in running out into the deluge to join them in the tiny building. He'd wait it out in the pickup.

What happened next would haunt Jonas for days, playing itself over and over in his mind. A horrendous crack of lightning hit nearby, and Jonas jumped involuntarily. Then he stared in shock as a blue-white ball of lightning started a short distance away and began following the barbed-wire fence bordering the ditch. The fireball flew down the metal fence, and when it reached Lightning, he reared high in the air, then fell to the ground with a horrible thud. Jonas screamed and flung open the pick-up door. Dashing past the still form of his horse, he followed his pounding heart to the cries inside the phone building.

Chapter 8

The Race

Jonas threw open the door to the small building to find his sobbing, soaking wet family. Terrified but apparently unharmed, Sue Ann and the children clung to each so tightly, they almost made the tiny cubicle look spacious.

"Daddy! Daddy! What happened?" Becca cried.

"The lightning hit close," Jonas answered, wrapping his arms around the dripping foursome. "Are you all okay?"

"I think so," Sue Ann said, wiping her wet face. "We're just so scared! Did it hit the trees right outside?"

Jonas didn't answer right away. He didn't want to frighten the children more than they were already, but he had to prepare them for what they would see when they went out.

"Daddy! Daddy!" Lydianne reached for her father. "Hold me!" Jonas picked up his four-year-old daughter and held her tightly. Sue Ann was sitting on the solitary stool in the building, rocking E.J., trying to stem his sobs. His eyes and nose were running unchecked, and Jonas reached into his pocket for his bandana. He wiped the youngster's nose and kissed his head. "It's okay, E.J. Daddy's here now."

The door was still standing open behind Jonas, and the rain had stopped as suddenly as it started. Becca looked out and her shrill cry told Jonas that she'd seen Lightning.

"Daddy! What happened to Lightning?"

Jonas's eyes met Sue Ann's, and he slowly shook his head. He set Lydianne down, drew Becca to him, and put his arms around both girls.

"Girls, Lightning got hit by that loud crash of lightning that you heard. I'm afraid he's dead," he paused and swallowed hard. For now, he had to be strong, he told himself. He could grieve later. "I know we're all going to be very sad, but the important thing is that we're all okay. Let's get into the pickup and go home."

Jonas took both of the girls' hands and led them out of the building. Sue Ann followed, carrying E.J. Both Becca and Lydianne began crying again as they passed the dead horse, but Jonas didn't pause as he walked with them toward the pickup. Once inside, with their children between them, Jonas looked at Sue Ann. Her white covering lay limp and damp on her head, but the wetness on her face was no longer from the rain. They'd all lost a member of their family, and it hurt. It hurt bad.

❖ ❖ ❖

The death of Lightning left more than emotional scars on the Bontrager family. It also left them without transportation. Lightning was their buggy horse. Without him, they had no means of travel.

As was always the case in times of disaster, Amish friends and family rallied behind the Bontragers. Jonus figured at least a dozen men offered him a horse to use until he could buy another one for himself. He remembered how the Amish had helped each other when a tornado tore through their community before he and Sue Ann were married. This was a much smaller disaster, but the feeling of concern and support was no less.

Jonas decided to accept a horse from Sue Ann's father. It was an older horse, very safe, and one they didn't use very much any more. Two days after the storm that killed Lightning, Jonas led another horse into the stall that had been Lightning's. He planned to put Lightning's halter on the mare and return hers to his father-in-law, but the sight of the old brown mare standing where his big bay gelding used to be kindled the sorrow Jonas had tried to ignore. Lightning had been with him for 14 years. They'd been through a lot together. Now he was gone.

Jonas felt the grief welling up inside, and this time he let it flow through him as he sat on a bale of hay, still holding the halter in his hands.

❖ ❖ ❖

More than they could have known when they accepted the train tickets to Indiana, Jonas and Sue Ann needed the brief escape that September. Mose's death, the loss of Lightning, the dairy herd responsibilities, caring for three young children—many factors had kept them emotionally and physically on the edge more than they liked to be. Plus, they didn't realize until they were on the train, just the two of them, how children had affected having time to just talk about things. It seemed like they were catching up for years as they rode the train through Kansas, Missouri, Illinois, and into Indiana. Somewhere in the Hoosier state, they started talking about the horse race Merv had told them about—the one Preacher would be in.

"Do you want to go along?" Jonas asked Sue Ann as they sat in the observation car, watching the countryside roll by.

"Yes," she answered. "Do you think we'll get in trouble?"

"Well, we couldn't do it back home, that's for sure," Jonas said. "But I don't see how it's any different than people going to Branson and Silver Dollar City."

"We Amish can go on vacation and take in some of the sights and entertainment, but when we're at home, it's illegal. That's something I've never understood," Sue Ann mused. "I suppose there's a good explanation for it, though."

Chapter
8

"Maybe it's because we aren't supposed to let our daily lives be invaded with that kind of thing. But once a year, what's it going to hurt?" Jonas offered.

"I don't envy the bishop who has to interpret the *Ordnung* and keep the community in the rules and standards," Sue Ann said thoughtfully. "I don't envy the ministers who are waiting right now for when we make bishop next month."

"Me neither," Jonas agreed.

❖ ❖ ❖

Jonas could feel the curious stares of the people around them as he, Sue Ann, and Merv walked toward the gates of Roppland Downs. It was a small racetrack—the purses for the winners weren't very big, but then neither were the entry fees. It was a place for smaller stables to participate in the racing scene, and for large stables to send their secondary horses. It reminded Jonas of going to the county fair when he was running with the young folks—just a lot of regular people hanging out and having a good time.

Of course, there was one major difference. Most of the people who came to Roppland Downs brought betting money with them. Watching a horse race was fine and good, but the opportunity to leave with more money than they came with—well, that's what made it intriguing. Jonas watched as the people lined up at the betting windows before going into the stadium. That was something he simply couldn't understand—putting out hard-earned money like that on what seemed to him to be a small chance at getting anything back. Not to mention that betting surely had to be unchristian.

Merv led them to a row of seats in the middle of the sta-dium, and handed Sue Ann a pair of binoculars. Jonas tilted his straw hat down to help keep the sun out of his eyes, and scanned the sandy oval track in front of them. The horses were starting to come out onto the track for their warm-ups.

"Is that Preacher?" Sue Ann asked, the black binoculars tight against her face. "The one that just stepped onto the track?"

"Yep, that's him," Merv confirmed.

"Jonas, look!" Sun Ann handed the glasses to her hus-band.

Jonas had spotted Preacher the minute he came into view. He thought he could see him just fine, but a shiver sprinted down his spine when he focused the binoculars for a close-up of the big black horse wearing number 10. Preacher was prancing impatiently under the tight rein of his jockey. The black body glistened in the sun, and the muscles in his hindquarters rippled with power. The binoc-ulars even brought the white spot on his chest into focus.

Jonas followed Preacher around the track as his jockey warmed him up. He handed the field glasses back to Sue Ann.

"What are his chances today?" he asked Merv with one ear on the announcer as he began to introduce the horses.

"It's a pretty strong field," Merv answered. "It's hard to say. You did put your money on him, didn't you?" he winked at the young Amish couple.

"Yeah, right," Jonas agreed. "Took my life's savings out before we came, and put it all on the line."

"Finally, we have number 10, Midnight Preacher out of Springdale Stables, with Gabby Cortez in the irons. Ladies and gentlemen, that's your field for today's race. And now, please stand for the national anthem."

Jonas took his straw hat off and reached for Sue Ann's hand as a single trumpet sent the strains of the national anthem through the loudspeaker system. The last notes were greeted with a roar from the crowd, followed by the announcement, "Two minutes to post for the Thorough-bred Maiden Stakes. Two minutes to post."

One by one, the horses were led into the metal starting gate stretched across the track. Jonas's heart jumped as Preacher entered his gate. He was the last horse in. A second later, the doors flew open.

"And they're off!" the announcer enthused. "It's Black Jack in the lead, with Go for Gold a close second. Rio Grande is in third, and Gimme a Buck's in fourth."

Preacher had drawn the outside starting gate, and his jockey was trying to bring him in closer to the rail.

"Come on, Preacher, get inside!" Merv was yelling. "Move him in, Gabby, move him in!"

Jonas's heart raced with Preacher as he watched the horse work his way into the thundering pack. The purple and green silks of Springdale Stables bobbed on top of the black horse, and Jonas reached for the binoculars.

"Coming into the quarter, it's still Black Jack in the lead," the loudspeaker related the action on the track. "Gimme a Buck's moved up to second, and Go for Gold's in third. Midnight Preacher's just taken fourth, followed by Rio Grande."

Sue Ann was screaming beside Jonas as the horses rounded the turn. "Go, Preacher, Go!" she yelled, her face flushed with excitement. "Oh, Jonas! Look at him!"

Of course Jonas was. He gripped the back of the seat in front of him, and accidentally touched the woman sitting there.

"Sorry," he apologized. She looked back and said, "That's fine." Then she looked again, and Jonas knew what was going through her mind. "Amish! Here!?"

The field was spreading out a bit now as they rounded the last turn. Black Jack was still holding his lead, but Gimme a Buck and Go for Gold had dropped back. When the horses reached the top of the backstretch, Preacher was in second place.

"Go, Preacher! You can do it!" Merv hollered. "Go get 'im!"

"You can do it, Preacher! Come on!" Sue Ann echoed, and she grabbed Jonas's arm. "He's going for it, Jonas, he is!"

And so it appeared. The stud colt that Jonas and Sue Ann helped welcome into the world on a moonlit night a little over two years ago wasn't giving an inch to the leader. In fact, the gap seemed to be narrowing ever so slightly. Jonas saw Gabby go for the whip, and ask Preacher for everything he had left to give.

"And down the stretch they come! It's Black Jack in the lead, and Midnight Preacher's coming on strong! The lead's down to one length, now a half, now they're nose to nose!" the announcer cried out. "It's Midnight Preacher and Black Jack! Neither one's giving! It's down to the wire! It's. . .it's too close to call! We've got a photo finish! Hold your mutual tickets, please, for a photo finish!"

"Do you think he did it?" Sue Ann clutched Jonas's arm.

"I don't know. My binoculars just weren't quite good enough to tell."

It seemed like a long time before the loudspeaker system finally blared, "We have the results of the Thoroughbred Maiden Stakes. Number 5, Black Jack, wins it, with number 10, Midnight Preacher, taking second."

"Oh," Sue Ann said. "But he did great, didn't he?"

"He did really good," Jonas agreed.

"Quite a finish there," the woman in front of them

turned and smiled at Jonas and Sue Ann. "You know that number 10 horse?"

"Yeah," Jonas said, stopping just before the wrong words slipped out. "Yeah, we know him."

Chapter
8

Chapter 9

𝓑𝓲𝓼𝓱𝓸𝓹

I t was hard to know who was more excited to see whom—
Jonas and Sue Ann to see their children, or the children
to see them when they returned from Indiana. When Jonas
and Sue Ann walked into Fred and Esther's house late that
evening in September, E.J. flew into his mother's arms as fast
as a 20-month-old can run. Lydianne, at 4, wanted to show
off the cookies she'd helped her grandma bake, and 7-year-
old Becca was full of questions.

"Did you see Preacher?" she wanted to know right away.
For Becca, the state of Indiana meant two things—her
Bontrager great-grandparents and Preacher.

Jonas and Sue Ann exchanged glances, and Sue Ann's
clearly communicated to Jonas, "You handle this one. It's all
yours."

"Well, yes, we did," Jonas answered his curious daughter. "He's doing very fine. Looking good."

"So when's he coming home?" Becca wondered.

Jonas knew his parents were listening to the conversation.

"Well, I'm not sure. 'Course you know we couldn't
bring him home on the train with us!" He laughed, skirting
the issue. But Becca wasn't giving up. "You said I could ride
him when he comes home, like I did in Indiana," she
pushed.

"I know, I know, Becca. It's just that some other people are riding him right now."

"Well, he's our horse. Why can't you take him away from them?"

"Just because. It's a long story. Now, no more questions."

"But Daddy!"

"Becca," Jonas's voice grew stern. "No more questions."

Jonas looked up at this father. He knew Fred had been watching him and taking in the whole conversation—he'd felt Fred's eyes, and he knew Fred was just as curious as his young granddaughter. The topic certainly wasn't closed.

❖ ❖ ❖

Early that Saturday morning, Jonas went to his parents' farm to help his father with his fieldwork. A number of years ago, when Jonas and Sue Ann were dating, the Amish community had split over whether to stay with horses for farming or switch to tractors. Jonas's father, Fred, had been one of the men who felt the strongest about remaining with horses, while Sue Ann's father, Cris, had decided to go with tractors. The result was that their parents ended up in different church groups, and Jonas and Sue Ann were forced to decide which church to join.

Jonas and Sue Ann had opted for the "horses" church. It hadn't made a difference in Jonas's vocation, because he worked for the Schmidt dairy and didn't farm for himself. It did affect him when he helped his father with his farming, because it meant working the fields with a team of horses or mules. It was quite a switch from the large equipment Jonas used at the Schmidt farm. Fred was hitching a team of six huge Belgian horses to the harrow when Jonas arrived that morning. Jonas unhitched the horse from his buggy and turned her loose into the pasture. The mare would have the day off while the Belgians had a lot of pulling ahead of them.

"You want the Belgians or the mules?" Fred asked as Jonas approached him near the barn.

"I don't care. Just put me to work," Jonas answered.

"My guess is you're more of a horse man," Fred said.

He's not wasting any time, Jonas thought. Now he'll ask about—"So what's going on with Preacher?" Fred's question came as Jonas predicted.

"He's racing. The stable's had him on the track this summer."

"Is he any good?"

"He's placed a few times. And he got second in a close one last weekend," Jonas walked around the horses for a last-minute check of the harness. Everything looked ready to go.

"Did you see the race?"

"Yep. Merv took us."

"I hope you put a lot of money on him," Fred said, and Jonas knew his father was kidding.

"I did," Jonas joked in return. "But then I put all my winnings on the next race—some horse Merv told me was a shoo-in—and I lost every penny."

Fred laughed. "Yeah, that's what happens when you gamble. Good thing we don't have a track here closer to home. You'd be there all the time."

"Yeah, like I could go if there was one here," Jonas replied, stepping onto the harrow and grabbing the long lines leading to the horses in front of him.

"Oh, you could go, but you'd probably get a visit from the ministers," Fred said.

"Just what I want," Jonas concluded the conversation. He knew his dad would pick it up again at the first opportunity. Right now, he had a field to work.

Fred brought the six large mules in from the corral and repeated the process he'd just gone through with the horses. Each mule needed a bridle, and then the heavy leather harness laid over his back and collar around his neck. The final step was attaching the reins that would enable Fred to guide the team as one unit. The whole process took an expert like Fred about 30 minutes. Then, walking behind the team as he drove them with the lines, he took them to where a second harrow sat in a line with his other farming equipment. He hitched it up, stood on the front end, and headed down the lane toward the field where Jonas was already working.

Chapter 9

Midway through the morning, the men took a break. Jonas was ready for it. At 30, he was strong and in his physical prime. But there was a big difference between riding in an air-conditioned tractor cab with push-button controls, like he did at the Schmidts, and standing on a bone-jarring, horse-drawn piece of equipment making its slow way through a dusty field. The difference was about 90 years. Or, in the case of the Wellsford community, a church decision.

"So, how long you gonna keep Preacher?" Fred picked up the conversation where he'd left it hours earlier. He and Jonas were resting at the end of the field, eating cookies and drinking water from their Coleman jugs.

"I don't know," Jonas answered.

"The longer he stays there, the less chance he'll ever be any good to you," Fred warned.

"Or," Jonas countered, "what if he runs for a few years and then we retire him out here? Knowing him, I think he'd settle right down."

"A stallion? Settle right down?" Fred laughed loudly and shook his head. "Not a chance. You know that."

"We could still cut him as a three-year-old. I've heard of it being done."

"Suit yourself," Fred said, standing up and taking a last long sip of water. "I think you're crazy. I think you should sell him while he's worth something to somebody else," he strode to his waiting team of mules.

Chapter
9

Jonas thought about Preacher while he balanced himself on the jerky harrow that morning and drove the Belgians back and forth through the field. His dad thought he should sell him. Certainly Springdale Stables would pay a good price for him, as well as he'd done in that last race. But some things were worth more than money, weren't they?

Wasn't it worth a lot to have a horse that he knew and trusted—one who'd known him and his family since the day it was born? With Lightning gone, wasn't it worth keeping Preacher for the potential he had to be a good family horse, both to be ridden and driven? Of course, he didn't know what Preacher would be like, now that he'd been on the track. But think how he'd look, and how they could fly, when Preacher was broke to drive! The thought made him smile. On the other hand, he might be a runaway. He might be uncontrollable. No, not Preacher. He'd be a good horse.

The conflicting thoughts whirled and tore through Jonas like a Kansas tornado, leaving behind the devastation of indecision. He hated not knowing what to do. Why couldn't he just sell Preacher like most "good Amishmen" would? Fact of the matter was, whether or not he kept Preacher wasn't entirely in his control. Depending on who the new bishop was, and how soon word got around about Preacher being on the track, he might be forced by the church to give him up. After all, Amish weren't supposed to own race horses.

Jonas was glad for a respite from his turmoil when Esther showed up at the end of the field, her hack buggy carrying a cooler filled with lunch for the men—cold chicken, potato salad, homemade bread, sliced tomatoes, and chocolate cake. A jug of tea came along to refill the jugs the men had taken that morning. The topic over lunch centered around one of the biggest concerns in the Amish community as the Sunday when they would make bishop drew near. Three ministers would be in The Lot—David Beachy, Leon Miller, and Eli Eash. David was young—about Jonas's age. He was liked by everyone, soft-spoken, and a farmer. David was still getting used to the idea of being a minister. The whispered word around the community was that he'd have a very difficult time if the role of bishop hit him.

Leon Miller, in his early 50's, owned the buggy shop in Wellsford. A businessman, he got along well with the public. Leon Miller possessed much more self-confidence than David, but some people thought he wasn't bishop material. Leon was one of the more progressive-minded church members, and there were those who didn't want that kind of person in the position of bishop.

Eli Eash was in his mid-60's and recently retired from a carpentry business that he'd turned over to his son. Eli appeared to be the best candidate, although there were those who said it'd be nice to have someone younger.

As Fred, Esther, and Jonas discussed the prospects, Jonas couldn't help but remember a conversation he and Sue Ann had with their neighbors Cindy and Matt Jacobs. Cindy and Matt were very aware of the upcoming event among the Amish, and Cindy had commented how strange she found it to be that the Amish leadership was chosen that way. "Our priests choose to go into the ministry," she'd said. "They feel called from God, and they get training to help with that calling. Your men just get hit with it."

Cindy's use of the word "hit" was ironic, because that's how the Amish described the happening. Jonas was sure that's how it felt to the one who opened the songbook to see the fateful piece of paper in it. Like a hit from an outside force that a person couldn't prepare for, but only react to.

But then, Jonas realized, the Amish believed that an Outside Force was involved. They believed that The Lot "falls on the man as the Lord decrees." There was biblical precedence for that method of choosing leadership. It had worked for centuries.

"…and Katie isn't saying much at all," Jonas heard Esther say. "When we asked her about it at the quilting, she just said, 'What will be will be.' I think she and David are both scared to death."

"I'm sure they are," Jonas agreed. He could imagine what was going through the minds of the young couple. It'd be as if he and Sue Ann were facing The Lot. He shuddered.

❖ ❖ ❖

They made bishop the first Sunday in October. Jonas felt the whole congregation holding its breath as the three candidates sat in front of the church, the stack of songbooks before them. He glanced at the three wives, each of them pale and drawn.

David Beachy reached for the first book. Jonas prayed the slip wouldn't be there. A gasp swept through the congregation, followed by a cry from David's wife, Katie.

The Lot falls on the man as the Lord decrees.

Chapter 10
The Return

David Beachy knew it was going to hit him, the talk in the community said. When church members arrived at his dairy farm that evening to do the milking for him, they found certain cows marked that were getting special feed or needed treatment for a health problem. David had marked them so someone who wasn't familiar with the cows could take care of them, the people said. David knew he was going to be made bishop.

Jonas headed up the crew that would milk and feed David's herd for the next week. Every morning and evening, Jonas and several other people from the church did David's chores. Meals were being brought to them, and the Beachys were being treated with the same care and attention the community would give when a death occurred in a family. David and Katie greeted their helpers and comfort-bringers with solemn faces and resigned spirits.

One evening during that first week, Sue Ann and the children went along with Jonas to the Beachys. While Jonas milked, Sue Ann and Katie prepared supper and visited quietly in the kitchen. The Bontrager and Beachy children played in the living room. David sat in a rocker on the screened-in porch, reading the Bible. His "seminary" classes had begun, and would consist of what he learned through personal reading and teaching from the other ministers.

Unfortunately, there'd been no opportunity to receive instruction from Moses, the past bishop, before his death.

After they'd eaten supper and the dishes were washed, Sue Ann and Katie played table games with the older children and read to the younger ones in the kitchen. The women knew the men might not want to be bothered.

Chapter 10

Jonas almost felt uncomfortable, being alone with David out on the porch. The light from the propane lamp inside filtered through the door, and a cool fall nip hung in the air. They made small talk for awhile about farming, but both of them knew it was covering up what was really weighing heavy on their minds. Jonas finally spoke.

"Did you know that morning?"

David didn't answer right away, and spoke slowly when he did. "Probably. I didn't sleep well the night before, and couldn't eat breakfast."

"And you marked the cows," Jonas stated.

"Yeah, that was connected to why I didn't sleep very good," David paused again. "I kept dreaming about my cows. They were out in the pasture, and it was time for them to come in. But they wouldn't come. They always come home at milking time. Bertha leads them. So finally I went out to get them," David was speaking faster now, as if he needed to tell the story, to get it out.

"I went to bring them in, and I found Bertha. She'd gotten twisted in some wire, pretty bad. Her leg was caught, and her udder torn. The other cows were standing around bawling because they knew it was time to go in. But they were waiting for Bertha to lead them."

"So, what happened?" Jonas asked.

"I kept trying to get her loose, and the barbed wire was cutting my hands too. The harder I worked, it seemed, the louder the cows were bawling. I finally woke up."

Jonas thought he knew why the dream had led David to

mark his cows for the milking, but he waited to hear it from him. The silence grew between them. After a long time, David spoke.

"I was afraid the cows were our church without a leader. I was afraid it meant I would get hit," David sighed loudly. "And you know the rest of the story."

"Yeah," Jonas said.

The men sat without a word passing between them, each lost in his own thoughts. Jonas's heart went out to the man beside him, a man no older than he but with the sudden responsibility of the church on his shoulders.

"David," he said, "Are you going to be all right?"

There was no answer. No answer except that, moments later, David buried his face in his hands, and his shoulders shook softly.

Jonas didn't know what to do or say. At least not right away. But as David's sobs lessened and he straightened up in his rocker again, Jonas leaned over and touched him lightly on the shoulder. "You *will* be okay, David. The Lot falls on the man whom the Lord chooses, and the Lord does not forsake the man he has called."

❖ ❖ ❖

When Merv Smucker's van drove on the Bontrager yard several days later, Jonas was glad to see Merv. Jonas knew Merv was around because he'd brought some relatives of David's from Indiana to visit him and Katie. Ever since the evening he'd spent with David, Jonas had been wanting to talk to Merv.

"Hello, Jonas!" Merv said, stepping out of the shiny, new, blue Ford van.

"Well, well," Jonas replied. "Amish-hauling must be good business! New van, huh?"

"Yeah, I finally did it," Merv patted the hood as he

came around the van. "The other one just had too many miles on it, and wasn't dependable any more."

"I bet you're here to see the filly—Preacher's sister," Jonas guessed, walking toward the horse fence. "She's a pretty one. The kids named her Black Beauty."

"Yeah, I've been wondering about her," Merv said, leaning against the fence. Patsy and the four-month-old filly walked slowly toward them. "She looks a lot like Preacher, except for those white socks. How's her temperament?"

"Good," Jonas said, scratching Beauty's neck. "Becca and the neighbor kids have been around her a lot, and she's been fine. I plan to sell her in a couple of months, when she's old enough to wean."

"Did you ever find out if she kicked Mose?"

"Nope, never did," Jonas grew serious. "But she's never been a problem since."

"Preacher's doing well," Merv said. "He had another win after the one you saw. The stable's impressed with him, and looking forward to next year. He'll be a very strong three-year-old."

"I've been wanting to talk to you about that. I want to bring him home."

"You *what? Why?*" Merv was incredulous.

"Word's going to get out. The last thing I want to do is make David have to deal with me owning a race horse. He's got enough to worry about as the new bishop."

"Then sell Preacher. I'm sure the stable would buy him."

"I've thought about that. But I've decided I want him back. I'll have one of the Petersheim boys break him to drive over the winter, and by spring he should be good and broke."

"I don't believe this, Jonas!" The anger in Merv's voice surprised Jonas. "He's had a good summer. You saw him!

We've put all this time and training into him, and he's look-ing good. Now you're just going to take him back?"

Jonas hated to upset Merv. Maybe he should reconsider.

"The stable owners won't like this one bit," Merv con-tinued. "You sure you have to do this?"

Jonas scuffed the ground with his foot. Finally, without looking up, he said, "Yeah, I do. I want him back."

❖ ❖ ❖

Two weeks later, on a beautiful fall Saturday afternoon, Merv drove in the yard again, this time pulling a horse trailer. Becca, Lydianne, and E.J. were playing "horse" out-side. Becca had a lead rope around her waist, and Lydianne was following along behind, supposedly telling Becca where to go. E.J. toddled along behind both of them.

When the children saw the truck and trailer, they ran inside to Sue Ann. "Mommy!" Becca shouted. "Somebody's here!"

"Where's E.J.?" Sue Ann asked immediately. "Is he still outside? You need to watch him when someone drives in the yard!" she said, running for the door, the girls close behind her.

Sue Ann saw E.J. the minute she got to the door. He was standing a few feet away from the house, his thumb in his mouth, his dark eyes large with wonder at the BIG THING on the yard. Seeing his mother, he pointed at the truck and trailer.

"Look!" he exclaimed.

Sue Ann bent down to her almost two-year-old son. "What is it, E.J.?"

Apparently in sudden need of his mother's security, E.J. drew close to Sue Ann, his eyes never leaving the bright white pickup and trailer. Merv had stepped out of the truck and was walking toward them.

"Hello!"

"Hi, Merv," Sue Ann answered, standing up with E.J. in her arms.

"Looks like the welcome party is ready," Merv said. "Becca, you know who's in that trailer?"

**Chapter
10**

"Preacher!" Becca screamed, and ran for the trailer. "Preacher's back!"

Preacher came out of the trailer much easier than he'd gone in when he left the Bontragers 16 months ago. Merv led the tall black stallion out of the trailer and across the yard to the horse shed. "Think I'll get him in a stall and let Jonas deal with introducing him back to the other horses," Merv explained. "He's a little different horse from what he was when he left."

"Let's go see him!" Becca ran for the shed.

"Becca! You come back here. We'll wait until Daddy comes home!" Sue Ann ordered.

Becca turned and began walking back reluctantly. "I'm just going to *look!*" she said. "Why can't I go see him?"

"Here, let me explain," Merv said. "Preacher's been—" He caught Sue Ann's eye and the vigorous shaking of her head before he could finish the sentence. "Preacher's been away a long time, and might not remember you," he concluded. "Plus, he's a lot bigger and stronger. It's better to wait till your dad is here."

"Jonas is helping his dad plant wheat," Sue Ann told Merv. "I don't know when he'll be back, but I'm sure he'll want to see you."

"I'll stop by later this evening," Merv said. "I need to head back first thing tomorrow morning."

Jonas arrived at home around 10 o'clock that evening, dirty and weary from a day behind the team of horses. Merv was sitting in the living room reading the paper when Jonas walked in.

"Well, hello!" Jonas said. "I come home and a strange man is in my house with my wife and kids."

"Yes, you're right," Merv stood to shake Jonas's hand. "But you should know, your wife and children have left me alone here while they take baths and get ready for church tomorrow."

"Good for them," Jonas chuckled. "I need a shower pretty bad myself right now."

"I won't stay long," Merv said. "Just wanted to let you know that I brought Preacher. The stable wasn't happy about letting him go, but he is your horse, after all. If you ever change your mind, let me know."

"I will," Jonas agreed.

"He's in the barn," Merv said, walking toward the door. "I need to get out of here so you can shower and go to bed."

"You think I'm crazy, don't you?" Jonas asked.

"Honestly? Yes," Merv looked Jonas in the eye. "But, like I said, he's your horse."

"I guess we'll see," Jonas said, standing at the door. "I think I know my horse. But we'll see."

Chapter 11

Becca

"Can I come along, Daddy? Mommy said I could!" Becca trailed Jonas as he left the house. They'd no more than come home from church, unhitched the buggy and changed clothes, and Jonas was heading out the door. The sunny October afternoon beckoned him outdoors, and he was more than a little eager to see how the big black stallion in the stall would react to being back home.

Jonas stopped and turned toward the seven-year-old. Becca's face had her mother's fine features and dark eyes, but Jonas recognized the spirit that burned within her as his own. Jonas found himself questioning life more than was often healthy for the mental well-being of an Amish person. More and more, Becca was doing that too.

"So, Mommy said you could, huh?" he slowed his stride to match Becca's. "And what else did she say you could do? Did she say you could ride Preacher too?"

Becca looked up at her father. He could see the moment of indecision in her eyes before she answered.

"I think she might have said that too," Becca said.

Jonas laughed out loud. "Becca, Becca, you know better than that. Mommy wouldn't ever give you permission to ride Preacher. We don't know if he's tame enough anymore."

"But he was in Indiana! I rode him there!"

Jonas and Becca had reached the combination buggy and horse shed and Jonas opened the door. Preacher eyed them alertly from the far corner.

"Hey, Preacher!" Becca exclaimed, running up to his door. "How are you?"

Jonas followed his daughter to the door, a lead rope in his hand. "Let's take him out," he said. "Just be careful to stay out of the way."

He didn't want to say anything too soon, but Jonas was happily surprised to see how calm Preacher was as he led him into the yard. He'd been dreading that Merv's predictions would be true—that Preacher was now too high-strung and hyper to be a family horse. Jonas had told Merv he thought he knew his horse. It looked like he was right.

Jonas led Preacher out to the lane and along the road, with Becca skipping barefoot beside them. Preacher's ears flicked back and forth and his eyes absorbed the countryside. October in Kansas meant the yellows and golds of the trees' fall foliage, the rusty red of fields of milo, and the just-peeking green of next year's wheat crop. A squirrel scampered across the road in front of Preacher. He shied, but only for a moment.

"Daddy, can I ride him now?" Becca stopped skipping long enough to ask her all-important question.

"Let's walk a little bit more," Jonas answered.

"Why was Preacher in Indiana?" Becca asked.

Jonas didn't answer. He didn't know what to say. If he told Becca that Preacher had been racing, without a doubt she'd tell her friends. Her friends would tell their parents, and the word would be out. Jonas's horse had been racing. Amish people didn't own race horses.

But, Jonas reasoned, Preacher was back home, and soon he'd be a buggy horse. Then the talk could stop. Preacher wouldn't be a race horse anymore, and Jonas wouldn't be doing anything illegal.

"Daddy, I asked you a question," Becca insisted. "Why was Preacher in Indiana?"

Jonas glanced down at his daughter's bare, dusty feet walking confidently on the sandy road. Except for school and church, she'd barely had shoes on since spring. He remembered those days as a child. When he'd asked the questions, and didn't have to be the adult with the answers.

"Preacher was being ridden in Indiana," he finally answered.

"Who was riding him? Somebody in that fancy barn?"

Jonas chuckled at Becca's recollection of the stable where they'd seen Preacher and his sire, Legacy.

"Yeah, somebody at Springdale Stables was riding him."

"Oh," Becca paused, and Jonas knew the questions weren't over. "Was there a little girl like me?"

"I don't think so."

"Who then?"

"Well, different people. One of them was a jockey named Gabby, I think." Jonas knew he'd committed to telling Becca the truth now.

"What's a jockey?"

"A jockey is a person who rides a horse in a race."

"Was Preacher in a race?"

"Yes, he was."

Becca stopped short in the middle of the sand road. She turned toward Jonas, hands on hips in her classic pose. "You mean Preacher was in a race and you didn't tell me?"

Jonas realized he could react defensively to Becca's accusation. As her father, he could "put her in her place." But something told him there was another way to relate to Becca—a way that might be better for them both.

"You're right, I didn't tell you," he agreed, stopping beside Becca. With Jonas taking a break, Preacher took the opportunity to munch on some grass in the ditch alongside the road. Jonas studied the shiny black horse beside him, then turned to look at Becca.

"I didn't tell you because the church says it isn't okay for an Amish man to own a race horse. That's why he's back here now."

"What's wrong with it?"

Preacher pulled on the lead rope, reaching for more grass in the ditch, and Jonas followed him a few steps. Normally, he wouldn't let a horse do that, but Preacher probably hadn't had a chance to graze on grass for a long time. Jonas decided to let him get by with it this one time.

"It's very complicated, Becca," Jonas answered her question. "But mostly what it's about is that racing would be worldly, and we Amish stay away from worldly things as much as possible." Jonas pulled lightly on the lead rope and Preacher dutifully turned to follow. "Let's head home."

"We could race home!" Becca said suddenly. "Me against you and Preacher!"

Jonas almost said no. It was the logical grown-up response. Instead, he grinned mischievously at his daughter.

"You? Against me and Preacher? Do I get to ride him?"

"No, silly, you have to run too!" Becca explained. "Ready? Go!"

Becca took off, her bare feet flying over the sand, her light purple dress flowing with her youthful body.

"Well, Preacher, let's go," Jonas encouraged, and began jogging after Becca. Preacher pricked up his ears as well as his hooves at this new kind of workout. He broke into a trot beside Jonas, his muscles rippling at the chance to stretch out.

Jonas figured they were about a fourth of a mile from home. Halfway there, he and Preacher were getting close to Becca, who kept looking behind her to see how close her competition was. As her father and the horse drew near,

Becca slowed to a stop.

"We're not there yet!" Jonas panted, jogging by with Preacher trotting behind him.

"I'm ... tired!" Becca yelled at the backs of her father and the black horse. "Stop!"

Jonas slowed to a walk. He didn't mind the excuse to stop running. Preacher, on the other hand, was just getting warmed up. He tossed his head and pranced impatiently at the new pace. "Whoa, Preacher, settle down," Jonas instructed, at the same time noticing that Becca was approaching the horse from behind. "Becca, stay back."

Becca gave the horse a wide berth. Preacher hadn't even broken a sweat on the short jaunt, Jonas noticed. He would soon, out of sheer impatience, if he kept this up. He'd tasted the freedom of exercise, and he wanted more.

"Whoa, boy," Jonas calmed. "Take it easy now. Whoa."

Preacher finally settled back into a walk, and the trio continued its stroll toward home. Jonas could see that Sue Ann and the other two children were watching them from the lane. As they approached, Lydianne came running out to meet them.

"Where were you?" she quizzed her sister.

"Down the road," Becca replied importantly. "We were just taking Preacher for a walk."

"Did you ride him?" Lydianne wanted to know.

"Not yet, but I will."

"How was he?" Sue Ann joined the conversation. She was carrying E.J., who wanted nothing more than to get down. Now.

"Really pretty good," Jonas said. "I can't wait to get him broke to drive. He's going to look so good pulling our buggy."

"You think he'll be calm enough?" Sue Ann questioned.

"I do. Look at him now. In fact, I think I'll finally give

Becca what she's been begging for," Jonas said, leading Preacher to the hitching post. He tied him up close to the cross bar, then turned to Becca with outstretched arms. "Come here."

Jonas lifted his daughter and gently placed her on Preacher's back, then turned to Lydianne. "You too, you want a ride?"

Lydianne's blue eyes grew big with surprise, and she smiled widely as her father lifted her onto the horse's back in front of Becca. "Now hold on!"

"Jonas? Are you sure..." Sue Ann's voice trailed off.

"It'll be okay," Jonas said. "We'll just go around the yard here a few times."

And so they did. Jonas found himself smiling a lot that afternoon. His horse was back. He wasn't ruined from racing. He was going to be a great buggy horse.

❖ ❖ ❖

The next day, Jonas took Preacher to the Petersheim boys to be trained to pull a buggy. Two months later, he was back in his stall at the Bontragers. He'd learned the nuances of pulling a buggy, and apparently his time on the track hadn't ruined him. Yes, he liked to run, but he was controllable. Jonas believed it was simply a matter of time and experience before Preacher would be completely reliable and dependable.

The last Saturday in January—it happened to be the day before E.J.'s birthday—Sue Ann asked Jonas if he'd go to Wellsford to buy groceries. The family would be having a birthday party the next evening, and Sue Ann needed ice cream and some other things from the local food market. Jonas decided it would be a great time to take Preacher to town.

A fresh layer of snow on the ground gave the Kansas

landscape a Christmas card look, and Jonas couldn't help but notice the contrast between his pitch black horse and buggy and the white world around them as he hitched Preacher up. It would be a beautiful ride into Wellsford, and Preacher seemed psyched to go too.

Jonas and Preacher had put about a mile behind them when Jonas noticed a car stopped along the side of the road ahead of them. As they drew closer, a woman stepped out of the car and aimed a camera at the approaching horse and buggy. Jonas sat back in the seat, away from the window, as the buggy rolled by the photographer.

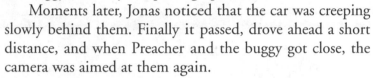

Chapter 11

Moments later, Jonas noticed that the car was creeping slowly behind them. Finally it passed, drove ahead a short distance, and when Preacher and the buggy got close, the camera was aimed at them again.

Normally fairly tolerant of "Amish watchers," Jonas was wondering what the deal was with this one. The car caught up with them again. This time, after passing them, the car continued down the road toward Wellsford.

Arriving in town a short time later, Jonas noticed the car parked on a side street. It followed him to the food market, and when Jonas stepped out of his buggy to tie Preacher to the hitching post, he came face-to-face with the photographer.

"I don't mean to offend you," the short young-looking woman said by way of introduction.

"No offense taken," Jonas said, not looking up from the lead rope he was tying.

"I know you don't like to have your pictures taken, but I wasn't really interested in seeing you anyway," the photographer continued. "It's your horse I was trying to get."

Jonas looked up. "My horse?"

"Yeah, he's absolutely beautiful. He doesn't look anything like the other Amish horses I've seen. And then, his black color against the snow ... well, I just had to try to get it on film."

"No problem," Jonas said. "Are you from the newspaper or something?"

"No, nothing like that. I just take pictures for fun. The good ones I print up and sell in gift shops."

"Oh," Jonas said, and began walking toward the store.

❖ ❖ ❖

Jonas couldn't get the episode with the photographer out of his mind, and it occupied his thoughts during the trip back home. He knew Preacher was one good-looking horse. In fact, he knew the Amish were talking about him too. Some were admiring him, and some were saying he looked too good to be an Amish horse. Whatever that meant, Jonas grumbled to himself. Sometimes this rules and regulations stuff got on his nerves. People could have immaculate houses and yards with everything in perfect shape, and that was okay. But get a horse that was "too fancy," and the tongues started to wag. Here he'd tried to stay in line and not give David Beachy anything to worry about as a new bishop. He'd brought Preacher home. Made him into a buggy horse. And now he looked too good.

A man can't win, Jonas shrugged as he turned into his driveway.

Chapter 12

A Dream

The morning after his trip into Wellsford and encounter with the photographer, Jonas hitched Preacher to the family buggy to go to church. Preacher had proven himself to be safe, Jonas felt. By 8:30 a.m. the family was climbing into the cold buggy.

"Girls, sit close together and I'll put the lap robe over you," Sue Ann instructed her daughters in the back seat of the buggy.

"Daddy, tell us the story about this robe," Becca said, picking at the dark brown hair on the large hide smothering their small laps.

"Tell us about the buffalo," Lydianne added.

"I will, as soon as we get going," Jonas said. Sue Ann had finished tucking the girls in and was now seated in the front with E.J. on her lap. Jonas wrapped a big comforter around his wife and son, then went to unhitch Preacher from the hitching post. He climbed into the buggy, took the reins in his hand and guided Preacher down the lane. As soon as they were on the road, he let Preacher set a steady pace that would get them to the home of David and Katie Beachy in about 40 minutes.

"Look!" E.J. laughed, puffing his warm breath into the cold air. "I smoking!"

The girls in the back seat giggled, and Jonas and Sue Ann

exchanged glances. "No, you're not smoking," Sue Ann responded. "You're just blowing air out into the cold. See, Daddy's doing it too."

"Daddy smoke?" E.J. wondered, looking up at his father.

"No, daddy doesn't smoke," Sue Ann said. "Where'd he learn this stuff anyway?"

"I think it was at the sale," Becca contributed. "Leon Miller was smoking. E.J. asked me what it was, and I told him."

"Oh," Sue Ann said.

"Who wants to hear the buffalo robe story?" Jonas changed the subject.

"I do! I do!" Becca and Lydianne chorused.

"Well, many years ago, at my birthday party when I was 16 years old, my Grandpa and Grandma Yoder gave it to me. Becca, if I'm 30 years old now, how long ago was that?"

Becca was quiet, then finally said, "I don't know."

"It was fourteen years ago," Jonas answered. "So that robe is older than all three of you kids put together. Am I right?"

"What does he mean, Mommy?" Becca asked.

"He means if you add up how old you three children are, the robe is still older than that."

Becca's silence in the back seat left only the soft sound of Preacher's hooves on the snow-packed road. Suddenly Becca blurted excitedly, "You're wrong, Daddy! We're 15! And that's more than 14!"

Jonas chuckled. "You're right! But so am I! You know why?"

"No, why?"

"Think about it. What have I told you about this robe before?"

"That it came from a buffalo."

"That's right. And how old was the buffalo?"

"I don't know."

"Well, let's say he was at least four years old when he died. How old did that make his hide before they tanned it and made it into a robe?"

"Four?" Becca answered.

"Right! So, if I've had the robe for fourteen years, and the hide was four before it got made into a robe, how old is it?"

"A hundred!" Lydianne enthused, eager to get in on the conversation.

"No, silly, not a hundred," Becca chided. "Is it 18, Daddy?"

"Absolutely right, my little mathematician," Jonas congratulated.

"Good job, Becca," Sue Ann added.

Feeling left out, Lydianne began to ask Sue Ann how old everyone and everything was that she knew—from her grandparents to Preacher to the doll she was holding. Sue Ann answered patiently, and Lydianne seemed to be running out of things to ask about when Becca interjected, "Daddy, the robe isn't that old."

Jonas had thought the robe discussion was long gone, but obviously Becca had still been mulling it over. "Why, Becca?" he asked.

"Because you said it was a hide they made into a robe. So the *robe* isn't that old," she said triumphantly.

Jonas turned to look back at the small face framed in its heavy, black Amish bonnet. His blue eyes met her confident dark ones, and he smiled. "You win," he acknowledged. This one might be a challenge as she grows up, he thought.

As the Bontrager buggy neared the Beachys, they came up behind a line of other Amish buggies. Jonas slowed Preacher down, but the big black horse didn't like the idea. He tossed his head and chomped on the bit impatiently, but

Jonas was firm. He would not pass the row of buggies. That would be rude and inconsiderate, and it just wasn't done.

❖ ❖ ❖

92

Chapter
12

That afternoon, as Preacher retraced his steps from the Beachys back to the Bontrager home, Jonas and Sue Ann discussed the news and gossip that had floated among the separate clusters of men and women during lunch. While each gender had its particular concerns and interests, they'd shared at least one topic in common. The bishop had announced that the congregation would have communion and "make minister" in one month.

Ever since David Beachy had moved into the position of bishop, the congregation had known that a minister would need to be chosen to replace him. The idea created a lot of apprehension among the members of the congregation, especially the married men. Any one of them could be nominated by someone in the congregation, and each man receiving three or more nominations would be included in The Lot.

"I wonder who'll be in," Jonas said thoughtfully to Sue Ann as the winter landscape rolled by them outside the buggy window.

"I bet your dad will be," Sue Ann responded quietly. "People like and respect him. Hasn't he been in before?"

"Once," Jonas said. "I think he will be again."

"How would he react if it hit him?"

"I think he'd be okay," Jonas said. "He has strong beliefs."

"But that's not all it takes," Sue Ann reminded. "He has to preach too."

"I know," Jonas said absentmindedly. He'd noticed a horse and buggy approaching from behind at a good speed. A closer look told him it belonged to one of the teenage boys—one who was known to have the fastest horse among the young folks. Jonas's heart quickened. That kid was assuming he'd go flying around the family buggy on its way home from church. Jonas would love to let Preacher give him a run for his money.

He wouldn't do anything risky, Jonas told himself. Not with his family in the buggy. He'd just let Preacher stretch out a bit more. He'd just keep the kid from catching him.

Jonas slapped the reins along Preacher's back, and the powerful horse responded immediately. Within moments he moved from a comfortable "Sunday afternoon" gait to a high-energy "movin' out" stride. Preacher loved to run, and he'd been given permission to do so, albeit within the limits of the reins and the bit in his mouth.

Jonas looked back. The young man's horse was obviously trying hard to catch them. Just as obvious, Jonas smiled to himself, was the fact that it wasn't happening. In fact, the distance between the horses was increasing. Jonas turned his attention back to the big stallion in front of him. Preacher was well under control, yet he was eating up the road in front of him with long hungry strides. Jonas glanced at Sue Ann. Her brow was furrowed, her mouth set in a firm line.

"Sue Ann? You okay?"

"I hope so," she said coldly. "But I'm not thrilled about being in a race with my family in the buggy."

"He's safe," Jonas assured. "Just look at him move!"

"Well, I don't feel that safe," Sue Ann held E.J. tightly on her lap.

"Okay, okay," Jonas said, pulling back on the reins. Preacher responded, although he made it obvious he didn't really want to. One-fourth of a mile later, he turned slowly into their lane.

Jonas was lifting Lydianne out of the buggy when the

horse that had been behind them careened into the yard. Jonas carried Lydianne to the house before going to talk to the teenage boy in the buggy.

"Some horse you've got there," the young man remarked.

"Yeah," Jonas acknowledged. "I hear yours is pretty fast too."

"He's okay. You wanna sell him?" the teen nodded toward Preacher.

"Naw, I don't think so."

"Well, he's somethin' else. Let me know if you ever change your mind," the kid said. "Let's go, Rex!" he turned his horse sharply around. The buggy tilted onto two wheels as it made the turn, then rattled down the lane behind the running horse.

Sue Ann and the children were huddled around the wood-burning stove when Jonas came in the house. Jonas added several logs to the stove and turned up its thermostat.

"Maybe we can all take naps after it warms up in here," Sue Ann suggested.

Ignoring the customary protests at the word "nap," Sue Ann laid several large comforters on the floor near the stove and invited her children to join her. Becca brought a book for Sue Ann to read to the trio. Jonas pulled up a rocking chair and began to read *The Budget*, an Amish newspaper covering news from Amish communities throughout the United States. It didn't take long before Jonas's head began to nod, and the newspaper slipped out of his hands.

Jonas was in a buggy being pulled by Preacher, and the horse was flying, absolutely flying. Loving every minute of it, Jonas knew without a doubt he'd made the right decision in keeping Preacher. Preacher was fast, safe, and he looked good. So very good.

Far in the distance, Jonas saw someone standing in the

middle of the road. As they got closer, Jonas recognized David Beachy. Any minute, Jonas expected David to step aside, out of the way of the fast-approaching horse. But he didn't. Jonas frantically tried to turn Preacher away, but he wouldn't waver. Preacher was going to run over David!

Seconds before impact, Jonas saw that it wasn't David standing in front of Preacher, but himself! He was about to be run over by Preacher!

In heart-pounding panic, Jonas finally stepped aside, and when he did, he found himself face-to-face with David. David's face was grave, and he was holding a Bible in his hands. He handed the Bible to Jonas.

"Daddy! Read!" Jonas woke with a start to see Lydianne standing beside his rocker, holding a book up to his face. He rubbed his eyes. The dream had been so real!

"Just a minute," he said quietly to the four-year-old. "Daddy needs to get a drink first." Jonas stood up and walked slowly toward the kitchen with Lydianne close behind.

Jonas filled a glass with water and took his time drinking it. The terror of the dream had subsided, but the images wouldn't go away.

Chapter 13
The Decision

For several hours after he woke up from his nap, Jonas felt haunted by the dream. It played over and over again in his mind, and he had trouble concentrating on his family. It was, after all, E.J.'s second birthday, and they would have a house full of relatives there for supper. He needed to get over it, he told himself.

The arrival of guests helped divert Jonas's mind, and he managed to laugh and have a good time. But later that evening, after everyone had gone home and the children were in bed, Sue Ann confronted him.

"What's the matter? You haven't been yourself since this afternoon."

Jonas continued picking up the toys scattered throughout the living room. "Oh, I don't know if I want to talk about it," he answered.

Sue Ann glanced at him as she stacked the clean dishes back into the cupboard. "Does it have something to do with how I reacted when you let Preacher run?"

"No."

"Are you sure?"

"Well, I guess it did have to do with Preacher running. But it was in a dream—when I fell asleep on the rocker this afternoon. Guess that'll teach me to sleep in weird positions," Jonas tried to make light of the subject.

"So what was it?"

Jonas sat down on the couch, one of E.J.'s toy horses in his hands. "I was driving Preacher, and we were going fast. He was doing great! But then David Beachy showed up in the middle of the road. He wouldn't move, and Preacher almost ran right over him." Jonas paused. Sue Ann left her dishes and came to sit down beside him.

"Then all of a sudden it was me that Preacher was going to hit. I stepped out of the way just in time, and there was David again. But this time he had a Bible in his hand and he was giving it to me. That's it."

"You're right, that is strange," Sue Ann agreed. "It's probably because you drove Preacher to church today, and I didn't like it when you let him run. David gave one of the sermons so that's where he comes in. Don't you think?"

"Probably," Jonas wanted to believe it was that simple. "What did David preach about this morning? I can't remember."

Sue Ann thought for a moment before responding. "He talked about *Gelassenheit*. Remember?"

Yes, now he did. *Gelassenheit.* The root of Amish culture and tradition. The idea of submission to a higher authority. Self-surrender, humility, yielding to God and to others. Never calling attention to yourself. He remembered it now. *Gelassenheit* was a common topic for sermons, and much of who he was and what he did as an Amish person grew out of it. *Gelassenheit* was their way of life.

"Yes, now I remember," he finally answered Sue Ann. "Well, anyway, it was just a dream. Let's go to bed." Jonas stood up and walked toward the stove to stoke it for the night. Something was nagging at him, especially now that he recalled David's words that morning. Something he needed to think about himself before talking to Sue Ann.

❖ ❖ ❖

Jonas didn't sleep well that night, and the 5:00 a.m. clanging of his alarm clock came as both a blessing and a curse. He flipped it off in the dark, then moved his hand to the switch on the battery-powered lamp on the table nearby. Dressing quietly in his long-sleeved cotton shirt and homemade barn-door pants, Jonas took a flashlight from the bed's headboard and turned the lamp off again. Sue Ann muttered a sleepy good-bye, and Jonas left for work at the Schmidt dairy.

At noon that day, Jonas was having lunch in the large farmhouse with Harlan Schmidt when a horse and buggy pulled into the yard.

"Somebody to see you?" Harlan wondered, a spoonful of chili halfway to his mouth.

"Looks like Edwin Keim's rig," Jonas peered through the window. He walked toward the door and opened it just as the doorbell rang.

"Hey, Jonas," a young Amishman about Jonas's age greeted him.

"Edwin! What brings you here? Come on in!"

"Thought maybe I could catch you here," Edwin said, then nodded in Harlan's direction. "Hello, Harlan."

"Hi, Edwin. Pull up a chair. Want some chili?"

"No, thanks. Wife's expecting me at home. Just stopped to ask Jonas about that stud horse of his."

"No, he's not for sale," Jonas laughed lightly.

"Don't wanna buy *him*. Just a part of him, you might say," Edwin chuckled in return. "I've got this mare. I was wondering if he'll be servicing mares this spring."

"Hadn't thought much about it. He's a thoroughbred, you know. Not a pacer."

"I know," Edwin nodded. "But I thought, with my standardbred mare, they might throw a great combination. With your horse's looks and speed, I'd think you could get quite a few mares comin' over."

"Maybe," Jonas half-smiled. "On the other hand, I hear a lot of people don't think he's a very good Amish horse."

"Well, maybe they're jealous," Edwin grinned. "Put me on the list, will ya?"

"I'll let you know."

Edwin left, and Jonas sat back down to his chili.

"So you've got quite the horse there, huh?" Harlan questioned.

"I guess so," Jonas said.

"Good thing you brought him back rather than selling him."

"Yeah," Jonas concentrated on breaking some crackers into his bowl of chili.

"Come on, Jonas, I've known you for fourteen years. You can say more than 'I guess so' and 'Yeah.' What's bugging you?"

Jonas sprinkled grated cheese over the crackers and chili. There was no way Harlan would understand what was beginning to jell in his mind.

"It's a long story," Jonas said. "I guess I'm not ready to talk about it right now."

"Suit yourself," Harlan closed the subject.

Suit yourself. Jonas heard the words reverberate in his mind. That was the problem.

❖ ❖ ❖

"I'm going outside for awhile," Jonas said abruptly that evening after supper with his family.

"Jonas?" Sue Ann wondered, the rest of her question hanging in the air between them.

"I'll tell you later," he said, slipping on his heavy coat and taking a Coleman lantern in one hand. The door slammed behind him.

Chapter
13

The snow had started to melt during the day, but what was left had frozen again and crunched beneath his shoes. A bright full moon flooded the yard as Jonas walked slowly toward the horse shed. He opened the door and hung the lantern on its hook. The horses looked up from their hay to see who was coming.

Jonas entered Preacher's stall from the inside door, and walked to the door on the opposite end—the one that opened into the corral. He unlatched that door and swung it wide. Preacher noticed the opportunity immediately, and sauntered out into the crisp winter night.

Jonas leaned up against the stall door and watched the muscular black stallion check out the moonlit surroundings. Colder, but a lot like the night when he was born, Jonas remembered. From the time he'd seen that wobbly black colt in the moonlight, he'd had high hopes for him.

And Preacher had never let him down. He was so proud of him.

Proud.

That was the problem. Pride was the stark opposite of humility. A proud person was everything the Amish were called not to be.

Looking back, Jonas knew pride had been creeping like a sinister snake into his being for a long time. At first, he was proud of Preacher. His appearance. His personality. His speed.

Then, when he brought Preacher home and broke him to drive, he was pleased to know that he'd been right about the horse. He'd never consider uttering the words "I told you so" to Merv or anyone else. But he had to admit, he'd thought them. It felt good to be right.

A coyote howled close by—close enough to make Jonas wonder if the coyote was watching him in the doorway. Soon a chorus of yips and coyote calls joined the first one. Preacher whirled to face the direction the howls were coming from, his ears alert, his nostrils flared.

Jonas felt the cold settling into him as he stood in the doorway. He grabbed a lead rope and curry comb from hooks on the wall and walked out to Preacher. Snapping the rope to Preacher's halter, Jonas led him to the fence and tied him up. Craziness, he thought, beginning to brush Preacher's neck and working his way down his legs. Crazy man is brushing his horse in the moonlight. Hope nobody goes by and sees this. But I've gotta do something to keep my blood circulating. And I've gotta think this through.

**Chapter
13**

Sue Ann was probably right about the dream, he mused. It could all be related back to the events of the day. What he hadn't been able to figure out was why Preacher was going to run over him. But now, after recalling David's sermon, he could see what it might mean.

Preacher had become too important. Instead of Jonas controlling him, he was controlling Jonas. Not in a mean or bad way, and through no fault of the horse. But in the subtle ways of the world. His speed made Jonas want to race, to beat the teenager's horse. His fine appearance made Jonas want to drive him to church, to show him off.

And what about the Bible? Why was David handing him a Bible in the dream?

Maybe because they'd be having communion in church. Maybe he wasn't right with God, or with his brothers and sisters. Maybe there was a stumbling block in his life.

Preacher.

Emotions flooded Jonas as he brushed the long black tail, and for awhile, the strands of hair seemed to swim together. As much as he couldn't imagine it, he knew what he had to do.

The decision made, he led the horse back into his stall, then slowly headed back to the light and warmth of his house and family.

Chapter 14

Good-bye

Jonas decided to talk to Becca, just the two of them, about his decision. She wouldn't understand—he didn't expect her to. But he wanted to be there with her if she got angry and frustrated. The next evening he asked Becca if she'd like to go out and feed the horses with him, and she eagerly agreed.

"I want to feed Preacher," she said, running toward the shed. By the time Jonas reached the building, Becca was carrying a can of grain toward the stallion's stall. He nickered when he saw the approaching can. That can meant a treat.

Becca set a bucket upside down next to Preacher's stall and stood on it so she could reach through to his grain box on the wall. She poured the can out, and then watched as Preacher ate. Jonas came up next to Becca.

"You like him a lot, don't you?" he asked.

"Yeah. He's my most favorite horse," Becca nodded.

"I like him too," Jonas paused. "But you know what, Becca? I think I'm going to let Preacher go back to Indiana to be a race horse again."

Becca turned on the bucket and stared at her father. The added height brought her eyes almost on the same level as his, and hers were spouting questions, confusion, and anger.

"WHY?" she cried out. "You said you like him!"

"I do, sweetheart, I do," Jonas put his arm around his

daughter. "It's hard to explain this to you, but I'll try. You know about us Amish staying away from worldly things, right?"

Becca nodded, but her eyes were fixed on Preacher.

"Well, that includes not having anything too fancy, or anything that will draw attention to us," Jonas paused. "Or anything that will make us feel proud."

Becca continued to stare at the horse in the stall. As Jonas watched, her dark brown eyes grew wet, and the tears spilled out. "Do you understand what I'm saying?" Jonas asked softly.

Becca sniffled. Jonas knew the wheels were working in her young mind. Finally she said, "But it's not Preacher's fault."

Preacher cleaned up the last bit of his grain and looked to Becca and Jonas for more. Becca stepped down from the bucket and got a slab of alfalfa hay. Jonas opened the door to Preacher's stall, and Becca put the hay in his feeder.

"No, it's not his fault at all," Jonas agreed, closing the door behind him and Becca. Becca was standing near the stallion, stroking his neck. "But maybe it will be better for all of us. Preacher will be happy to race again, I'm sure."

"Well, it won't be better for me," Becca cried, a fresh stream coursing down her cheeks. "I love Preacher, and you're taking him away."

❖ ❖ ❖

The next day, during his lunch break at the Schmidt dairy, Jonas called Merv in Indiana and told him he was ready to sell Preacher. Merv said he'd come pick him up, and Jonas said anytime would be fine, as long as it was before the second Sunday in March—the Sunday when they had communion and made minister.

That same day, on his way home from work, Jonas

stopped at the neighbors, Cindy and Matt Jacobs. He needed to tell the children that Preacher would be leaving, and he also had a request to ask of Cindy.

"Jonas! Come in!" Cindy met him at the door.

"Thanks. I'll only stay a few minutes," Jonas stepped inside and took his black hat off. "I need to ask a favor."

"Fire away," Cindy smiled. "Is Sue Ann pregnant? You're warning me about another trip to the hospital?"

"No, no, no, nothing like that," Jonas laughed. "It's about Preacher." He grew sober. "I'm going to sell him, and it's really hard on Becca. I was wondering if you could come take a picture of him, and give it to Becca."

"Of course I can do that," Cindy said. "But why are you selling him? I thought he was doing so well."

"Oh, he is," Jonas shifted uncomfortably. "Maybe too good."

Cindy's eyebrows went up, and Jonas sighed to himself. This was the worst part, he thought. The explaining. At least Cindy had been around the Amish long enough to kind of understand their ways. Well, maybe not understand. More like accept them for who they were.

Jonas briefly explained why he was selling Preacher, and while he was talking, Ben and Marie came into the room. Jonas broke the news to them, but their reaction wasn't as strong as Becca's. Their intrigue and interest with Preacher had waned when he went to Indiana the first time, and they'd spent very little time with him after his return. Still, they wanted to come say good-bye when Merv arrived to pick up Preacher.

❖ ❖ ❖

The decision to sell Preacher wasn't the only thing on Jonas's mind during that February. It happened that Jonas and Sue Ann's turn to "take church" was the second Sunday in March—the day of communion and choosing of a minister. Their house, buggy and horse barn, and yard would get a top-to-bottom, thorough cleaning. The day before the service, the furniture in the house would be moved out to accommodate the rows of church benches. Food had to be purchased and prepared to serve the 30-some families for lunch, and church cookies baked for the children during the service. Sue Ann had a list of things to do, and a time frame to do them in.

Chapter
14

The last week in February was the time to clean the house. Sue Ann's mother and sisters were scheduled to come over to help with the cupboard-by-cupboard, room-by-room task. The night before they would all be there, it started to snow.

It snowed all night. It was still snowing in the morning when Jonas got up to leave for work, and when he stepped outside into the darkness, the snow covered his boots. His flashlight revealed a world drowned in white, and Jonas knew he wouldn't be going anywhere in the Schmidt pickup. He turned around and retreated to the house. It didn't look like Sue Ann would be getting much help with housecleaning today either. At least not from anyone who needed to use the road to get there.

Jonas lit the propane lamp in the kitchen and sat down at the table. Maybe he could catch up on some reading. And then there was that circle letter he needed to answer.

Circle letters were common ways of communication among Amish friends and relatives. Without phones, faxes, or computers with e-mail, the Amish still relied on the postal system to keep the ties going between people in different parts of the United States. A circle letter consisted of a group of families that wrote their news in a letter, added it to the other letters in the packet, and sent it on to the next family in line. Jonas and Sue Ann were in several circle letters. It was fun to read what was happening in the lives of the other people, but it was always a challenge to get their own written. Jonas decided to re-read the letters in the packet before beginning his.

"Been quite a winter here," Jonas read the neat printing of his cousin's wife in Michigan. "Had a big snow on November 1, and it hasn't let up much since. We missed having church two Sundays in a row. When we finally had it, we made minister. It hit Kenny King. They'd been thinking about moving to Oklahoma, but I think they're going to stay here now."

Sue Ann walked softly into the room and came to stand behind Jonas's chair, putting her arms around him from the back. "Good morning, Honey," she said. "You couldn't go to work because of the snow?"

"Yeah," Jonas said. "And I don't think your mom and sisters will be here to help you today either."

"Hmm … mmm …" Sue Ann mused. "They can't get here, and you can't get out, and we have a house to get ready for church. I wonder what that means."

"Oh, no," Jonas groaned. "Surely you wouldn't trust me to do it good enough."

"Surely I might have to," Sue Ann laughed lightly. "But you can write the circle letter first, while I make breakfast."

"Did you read this? Kenny King got made minister in Michigan."

"Yeah, I saw that. He'll do okay," Sue Ann commented. "I wonder who it'll hit here," she paused. "Do you still think it could be your dad?"

"Who knows?"

"Well, whoever it is, we need to have this house ready," Sue Ann said.

❖ ❖ ❖

The snowstorm lasted the rest of that day, and then a cold north wind came in to blow the snow around into tall impassable drifts. While other homes in the community struggled without electricity and heat, the Amish were cozy with their wood heat and propane lights. Jonas and Sue Ann worked together, "assisted" by the three children. Becca took it upon herself to clean the room she shared with Lydianne. "It wouldn't be nearly as much fun if we'd asked her to do it," Sue Ann smiled wryly as Becca marched off with her assortment of cleaning supplies.

"You got that right," Jonas agreed, standing on a chair, washing soot from the wall behind the stove.

After leaving Kansas covered and temporarily immobile, the winter storm moved northeast, blanketing Missouri and Illinois before finally losing its punch in Indiana. Merv still hadn't come to pick up Preacher, and Jonas found himself getting antsy. He'd made the decision several weeks ago, and he just wanted to get it over with. He'd told Merv to come before the second Sunday in March. Now the storm would probably keep him from trying to make the trip.

On Saturday morning, the day before church at their home, Jonas hitched Preacher to the buggy and went to get the church wagon. The square box-looking wagon contained the church benches, and it traveled from one home to another for the services. He returned several hours later, pulling the wagon behind the buggy. The white-with-green-trim pickup and horse trailer of Springdale Stables stood in the Bontrager yard.

"So, you made it after all," Jonas greeted Merv as he got out of the buggy. "Snow storm hold you up?"

"Yep," Merv agree. "But I finally got here."

Jonas unhitched Preacher from the buggy and clipped a lead rope to his halter.

"Think I'll walk him a little, cool him down before he has to stand in that trailer for 16 hours," Jonas said. "I bet Sue Ann would have some fresh cinnamon rolls and coffee for you if you hint hard enough."

"Sounds good to me," Merv smiled, walking toward the house.

Jonas led Preacher up and down the lane several times, and the finality of the moment began to sink in. This was the last time to look into the alert bright eyes of the horse he'd known since his birth; the last time to stroke the shiny black coat with its small star of white; his last time to lead 1,300 pounds of power and personality named Preacher. Somehow, it just didn't seem fair.

The back door of the house slammed, and he saw Becca running toward them. Jonas stopped, and Becca buried her face in the sleek black neck. "I love you, Preacher," she cried. "I'll never forget you."

The small Amish girl and the tall stallion seemed frozen for a moment in the winter stillness. Jonas swallowed past the lump in his throat, and waited.

Jonas was glad for the distraction when Sue Ann came out of the house, holding the hands of Lydianne and E.J. They were bundled from top to bottom, and squinting in the sun-on-snow glare. "Did you come to say good-bye to Preacher?" Jonas asked, picking up E.J.

"Bye, Peecher," E.J. waved his mittened hand.

Hearing her family, Becca finally left Preacher's side and went to stand by her mother. Sue Ann enfolded Becca with one arm. "He's going to be a great race horse," she said. Becca nodded, and swept the sleeve of her coat across her face.

Chapter 15
The Lot

"Becca, you'll need to help take care of the children today," Sue Ann said as the family sat down for a quick breakfast at 6:00 the next morning. "You won't be with us because we're having communion. You and the other children can play outside or in the basement. Okay?"

Becca nodded as she took a spoonful of cereal. "How long will it be?"

"All day," Jonas answered. "We're making minister after we have communion, so it'll be late in the afternoon before we're out."

"Who'll feed us?" Becca wanted to know.

"Some of the older girls will get the food for you," Sue Ann explained. "You'll eat in the basement."

"Do I have to watch E.J.?"

"The older girls will take care of him, but you can help. He knows you," Sue Ann said. "Now, let's get you all cleaned up and dressed."

By the time the breakfast dishes were washed and the family dressed for church, the buggies of early arrivers were already rolling into the yard. Jonas's parents, Fred and Esther, were the first to show up so they could help with last-minute preparations. As Jonas greeted his father, he couldn't help but look at him with a mixture of respect and empathy. Fred would surely be named to be in The Lot,

Jonas speculated. By the end of the day, his father could be a minister. May God be with him, Jonas thought. Or with whoever gets hit.

The communion observance began at 8:00—earlier than a usual church Sunday. But there was much ground to cover, as the ministers traced the Old Testament story, followed by the New Testament, in their sermons. The morning hours moved slowly. Jonas tried to concentrate, but his mind wandered often. Several times he almost fell asleep, catching his head as it began to drop. He shifted his position slightly on the backless bench, but there wasn't much room to move—the congregation was packed tightly into the rooms of his house.

At midday, people began taking turns slipping out of the service to eat a quick, light lunch in the basement. Unlike a normal Sunday, when the meal was a time for socializing and community-building, a break to eat during this service would be disruptive. The service was building to a point, a pinnacle of commitment and communion, and nothing should prohibit that flow. With several ministers giving sermons, the preaching continued nonstop.

Jonas was one of the last to eat, and he thankfully left his seat for the brief escape. He desperately needed to stretch, and his stomach had been complaining for the last hour or so. As he silently ate the simple meal of sandwiches and Jell-O in the basement with the others in the last group, he watched the children seated on blankets in one corner of the room. A girl of about 13 or 14 was reading to a small group of toddlers, including E.J. Jonas knew the hope was that the children would fall asleep and take long afternoon naps. Isn't it ironic, he smiled to himself. Down here she's trying to get them to sleep, and upstairs we'll be fighting the temptation to doze off. He stood up and slowly made his way back to his place in the living room.

The last of the ministers was talking, which meant bishop David Beachey was next in line. Jonas wondered how he'd do, this being his first communion sermon and service. He knew David had spent a lot of time reading and memorizing in preparation for this Sunday. The mental stress must be awful, he thought.

David began his sermon where the minister before him had left off, reiterating that the hidden sins of pride and disobedience will destroy not only the person who harbors them but also the church.

"The grain of wheat must be broken to become flour for bread," David said. "The grape must be crushed before it can become wine. We too must be broken and crushed to be a part of the body of Christ. Pride has no place among us. To be humble and obedient, that is what Jesus Christ asks of us."

There it was, the often-heard warning against pride, Jonas thought. The reason he'd felt he had to sell Preacher. Hard as it had been, he was glad he did it.

David continued for another hour, recounting the sacrifice and bitter suffering of Christ, holding him up as a model for all to follow. As he told the story of Christ's crucifixion and death, David's voice broke several times. Jonas felt it was both the strain of presenting the message as well as the story itself that was affecting David, and his heart went out to him.

David moved from his sermon into the communion service itself, taking a loaf of bread and breaking it. He served each member a piece as they came before him. After the taking of the bread, a single cup of grape wine was passed through the congregation.

The final aspect of the communion ritual was foot-washing. The ministers placed several basins of water and towels in the rooms. The congregation was already segre-

gated by sex in its seating, so for the foot-washing, pairs of men and pairs of women went to separate basins to dip, wash, and dry each other's feet.

Jonas was seated next to Edwin Keim. As their turn drew near, they removed their shoes and socks, then approached the basin together. Edwin sat down, and Jonas stooped to take one of his feet. Placing it in the basin, he washed the foot, took it out, and dried it. As he repeated the process on the second pale white foot, he couldn't help but remember that ankle—the one Edwin broke when he fell out of a barn at a young folks party in Missouri. Yes, we've been through some things together, Jonas thought.

The men exchanged places, and as Edwin washed Jonas's feet, Jonas remembered a more recent encounter with Edwin—the day he stopped at the Schmidts to see if he could breed his mare to Preacher. He'd have to tell Edwin he sold the stallion.

Jonas felt guilty for letting his mind stray. Edwin was drying his foot. That done, the men stood and exchanged a "holy kiss," gave each other a blessing, and walked back to their seats.

The foot-washing completed, the service moved directly into the choosing of a minister. Bishop David and the deacon went to Becca and Lydianne's bedroom, where they sat on chairs and took the names of nominees from members as they came into the room one by one. Jonas could feel the tension beginning to collect inside the house as he waited his turn, and he struggled with whose name he would put forth. He wanted to say "Fred Bontrager." He would be a good minister. But did he wish that upon his dad? And would the deacon and bishop think him vain to be naming his own father?

Finally, with the deacon and bishop and the decision before him, Jonas said "Fred Bontrager."

After what seemed like a long time, in a day that had already stretched into its eighth hour, the deacon and bishop emerged from the girls' bedroom to read the list of names that would be in The Lot.

"Reuben Keim. Sammy Miller. Fred Bontrager," Bishop David recited. "Gideon Eash. Jonas Bontrager. Lyndon Schrock."

Jonas's heart jumped and began racing. No. No! It couldn't be! Who would name him? Why? Why would anyone suggest *him*? He was too young, too full of questions, too rebellious! Surely he heard wrong!

He could feel eyes upon him, and he knew he'd heard right. Reuben. Sammy. Fred. Gideon. Lyndon. Him. Six men in The Lot. At least there were six. Better than three, or four. It wouldn't hit him. God knew better than that. It couldn't hit him.

Jonas stood up and worked his way out of the row where he was sitting. He knew his face was flushed. The knot that had started in his stomach when he heard his name was beginning to tighten. He knew everyone was watching him. Him and the five others.

A table and six chairs were brought to the front, and the candidates stood in a row before Bishop David. "When you were baptized, you pledged to serve the church if called," he began. "I ask you now if you are in harmony with the ordinances of the church and the articles of faith."

One by one, the men quietly answered, and with trembling conviction, Jonas responded "yes."

"Please kneel," David instructed, and as the six men obeyed, David prayed for God to show which one he had chosen.

After the men stood up, the deacon walked into the room and laid six songbooks on the table. The men took chairs around the table, and when they were seated, David intoned, "Lord of all generations, show us which one you have chosen among these brethren."

Jonas's hands shook as he reached for a songbook. They would open them in order of age. He would be second to the last. By then, someone else would have the Bible verse in his book. Somebody else would get hit. His father. Surely it would be his father.

Chapter 15

The first songbook was empty. Likewise, the second. Fred was next. He opened the book. Empty.

Jonas couldn't believe it. Not only had Fred escaped, but there were only three books left! The tension in the house tightened, even as audible sighs of relief escaped from the wives of the first three men.

Beside Jonas, Gideon took a deep breath and flipped through the pages of his book. Empty.

And now it was Jonas's turn. He gulped, and allowed the well-worn songbook to fall open. There, nestled in the middle— a white slip of paper.

Jonas's clammy hands went to his face, and his head dropped down. He felt arms around him from behind, and was conscious of cries in the congregation. He couldn't believe it. He'd been hit. He was now a minister. Minister for life.

❖ ❖ ❖

Later that evening, Jonas and Sue Ann sat in their living room, surrounded by family members and close friends. Fred and Esther were there, as well as David and Katie Beachy. Jonas noticed that Sue Ann's dark brown eyes, usually full of life and energy, were heavy with shock and resignation. He felt as emotionally drained and empty as she looked.

Jonas was thankful for the understanding and comfort that David and Katie could give. They'd been through this, not once, but twice—when David was made minister, and then bishop. They knew the heaviness of being hit in The Lot. They understood the feelings of inadequacy, yet the belief that God had called a leader. They could do more than offer sympathy; they could offer encouragement and hope.

"I'm going out for some fresh air," Jonas announced when the atmosphere in the room began to get to him. Between the somber attitudes of the well-wishers and the keyed-up children, who couldn't comprehend what was going on, he needed some space. He picked up a flashlight, stepped out into the cool March evening and began walking toward the barn. He heard someone behind him, and turned to see David.

"Mind if I come along?" David asked.

"Fine with me. It was just getting to be too much in there," Jonas said.

"I know."

Reaching the barn, Jonas opened the door and stepped inside. The horses didn't need to be fed—someone from the church had taken care of the chores that evening. He just needed to get away, and this was one place to go. He could hear the two horses munching on their hay, but the last stall was silent. Preacher's stall.

"I sold Preacher yesterday," he said to David beside him.

David was quiet for some time, and then he asked. "Did you know?"

"No." Jonas stated emphatically. Long moments passed in the dark with only the sound of the horses. "At least, I don't think so."

"Then why'd you sell him?"

"It was just something I felt like I had to do."

David didn't respond, and Jonas knew what David was

thinking. Gradually, he began to realize it too. There was a reason he'd sold Preacher before today. A Power greater than him had been involved. David broke into Jonas's thoughts.

"Jonas, remember what you told me when I was made bishop? You said 'The Lot falls on the man whom the Lord chooses, and the Lord does not forsake the man he has called.' Remember?"

"Yeah."

"It's true. Take my word for it, Jonas. It's true."

Chapter 15

118

Chapter 16

Destiny

J onas didn't go to work the next day. He wasn't expected
to. In fact, he was expected *not* to go. Someone in the
church stopped to tell Harlan that Jonas wouldn't be at
work for at least several days because he'd been made minister. Family and friends would be bringing in meals and
spending time with the Bontragers during this period of
adjustment to Jonas's calling.

David and Katie arrived around noon that day, bringing fried chicken and all the trimmings. After they'd eaten
and washed the dishes, the two young couples sat on the
porch and talked.

"You'll have to read your Bible a lot," David said to
Jonas. "I don't know about you, but my German-reading
wasn't very good before I was made minister. I spent a lot of
time learning it for church."

"Dad tried to get us to read it," Jonas replied. "I just
had no idea I'd need it someday."

"Well, you do now, but you'll get the hang of it. Take
time during these next few days to get started. You'll have
to give a response in church next time."

"In just two weeks," Jonas said quietly.

"Yeah," David agreed. "You're lucky you have such a
good wife by your side. I know she'll do everything she can
to help you."

"I'm not sure what I *can* do," Sue Ann said.

"Give him space when he needs it, and keep the kids out of his hair when he's reading," Katie suggested.

"Understand him when he seems moody because he's probably got a lot on his mind," David added.

"She knows how to handle me," Jonas half-smiled. "I'm always the one asking questions, and she keeps me in line. Don't you, Honey?"

"I don't keep you in line, Jonas. We just talk and think things through together."

"That's exactly what I mean," David nodded. "You'll need to do that, and that's why you're lucky to have Sue Ann. I don't know how I'd have gotten through being made minister and bishop if it wasn't for Katie."

"It still seems unreal that it hit me," Jonas said. "I thought all along it would be my dad."

"People are going to ask you if you knew," David warned. "You'd better think through what you're going to say, because it gets talked about."

"I have thought about it. Last night, after you left. I realized that when I decided to sell Preacher, I had this feeling that I *had* to sell him, and that it *had* to be before that Sunday. I didn't know why it seemed so urgent, except that he was too fine-looking, and I was being proud of him," Jonas paused. He felt he was exposing himself, bit by bit, to the others on the porch with him. He hadn't even had time to share these thoughts with Sue Ann until now.

"Maybe it was God warning me," he admitted. "It wouldn't be fitting for a minister to have a flashy horse," he waited again for the thoughts and words to formulate in his mind. "'Course I could have sold him as soon as it happened."

The two couples sat in silence as a cardinal sang from one of the nearby cottonwood trees, and then a slow chuckle began working its way through Jonas. "Good thing I sold Preacher before Sunday, 'cause now he can be a race horse. I might have felt more guilty selling him back to the stable after I was a minister."

Sue Ann, David, and Katie all turned toward Jonas. Sue Ann's eyes were the first to light up with mirth; David's and Katie's smiles soon followed.

"Sue Ann, I may need your help keeping him in line," David grinned wryly.

Sue Ann reached over and laid her hand on Jonas's knee. "Just what I've been waiting for—an excuse to tell him what to do," she laughed softly. "But I'm still not sure it'll work."

❖ ❖ ❖

It was hard for Jonas to say whether that spring and summer felt like they passed quickly or dragged on for an eternity. Between his work at the Schmidt dairy, helping his father farm, and the new responsibilities of being a minister, the time flew by. Certainly church Sundays seemed to come faster than ever before.

On the other hand, the hour or so that he preached during each service seemed to last for days. Without notes to follow or guide his sermon, Jonas could only rely on what came to mind from memory. Certain sermon themes were repeated by Amish ministers time after time, and Jonas picked up on those topics. He read his Bible during the weeks and tried to find ways to incorporate what he read, what he'd learned from ministers before him, and what he himself brought to the theme. It wasn't easy.

It wasn't easy, but Jonas found himself surprised at the way he and Sue Ann were adjusting to his new role. He could now say, from personal experience, that the words he'd given David, and that David had shared with him in return, were true. The Lord was standing with him.

On the first weekend in September, over Labor Day, a large Bontrager reunion was scheduled to happen in Indiana. Jonas and Sue Ann decided to take the children and join a van-load of relatives that was going from the Wellsford community. It'd be good for the kids and their great-grandparents to see each other again.

The van arrived in the Indiana Amish community on a Friday evening for the two-day reunion. The next morning, Merv showed up at the retreat center where the family gathering was being held. He talked to Jonas for a few minutes, and then left. At his first opportunity, Jonas pulled Sue Ann aside.

"Merv stopped by," Jonas said. "He wants to take us to see Preacher race tomorrow afternoon. He says he's doing great and we've gotta see him."

"Oh, my goodness," Sue Ann said, her hand moving involuntarily to her mouth.

"Yeah," Jonas agreed. "What shall we do?"

"When do we have to decide?"

"He's stopping by tomorrow to either pick us up, or not."

Somehow, Jonas knew deep inside that he, Sue Ann, and their children would end up at Roppland Downs that Sunday afternoon, and they did. Minister or not, he figured this was the last chance for him and his family to see Preacher run. If he got flak, he'd deal with it.

If Jonas had felt eyes on them a year ago when he and Sue Ann attended the races with Merv, the curiosity-quotient seemed to have increased three-fold with the addition of their children. He knew he felt more guilty too, so the stares burned harder. He was glad when the family found a place to sit in the crowded stands.

If the onlookers were curious about the Amish family,

the Bontrager children were certainly equally intrigued with their surroundings. Becca was beside herself with excitement at the chance to see Preacher in a race. Lydianne was taking it all in with her big blue eyes, and E.J. squirmed in his father's arms. "Down," E.J. insisted. "Down!"

"Look at the horses!" Jonas tried to direct the boy's attention to the parade of horses on the track.

"Is Preacher out there?" Becca wanted to know. "Where? I don't see him!"

"There's another race before his," Jonas explained, setting E.J. down between him and Becca. "You can be down, but you stay right here," he told the youngster.

"Sue Ann, do you have the binoculars Merv gave us?" Jonas asked. "Let's give them to the kids to watch this race."

"Sure!" Sue Ann dug around in E.J.'s diaper bag. "Here, Lydianne, look at the horses through these. Stand up here beside me."

Lydianne climbed up onto the wooden seat and Sue Ann held the black binoculars up to the little girl's face. Lydianne took them in her hands and exclaimed, "Oh! Look!"

"Let me see!" Becca begged, stepping up on the bleacher beside her sister.

While the girls enjoyed the race through the binoculars, Jonas and Sue Ann watched with one eye on the horses and the other on E.J.

"It won't be long now until Preacher's race," Jonas said after the winner had been to the winner's circle for the awarding of the trophy and picture-taking. "Watch the gate back there for when the horses come onto the track."

"All horses for Race 12, the Thoroughbred Handicap, to the paddock," the loudspeaker system blared. "Fifteen minutes to post time. All horses for Race 12 to the paddock."

Jonas caught Sue Ann's eyes, and they smiled. Whether or not they should be here, they were, and it was exciting.

"Where is he, Daddy?" Becca asked, the binoculars pasted to her face. "Nobody's coming."

"Pretty soon."

Finally, the announcer broke the news the Bontragers had been awaiting. "Riders are up and the horses are coming onto the track. In the number 1 position, Grady's Gold, owned by Gravel Ends Ranch, with Victor Rojas in the irons. In the number three…"

"What's it mean, 'in the arms'?" Becca asked.

Jonas couldn't keep from laughing as he answered, "It's 'irons', 'in the irons' and it means that the jockey's feet are in the iron stirrups. Listen!"

"Number four is Midnight Preacher, owned by Springdale Stables, with Gabby Cortez in the irons."

"Preacher!" Lydianne screamed. "Let me see!" She grabbed the binoculars away from Becca.

Jonas couldn't stop the smile that spread across his face as the big black stallion pranced onto the track. Preacher—his Preacher—wow!

Jonas studied the large wagering sign across the track from the stands. The odds on Preacher to win were 5:1.

"A lot of people are betting on him," Jonas said to Sue Ann. "If not to win, at least to place in the top four."

"One minute to post," the announcer declared.

Preacher's jockey in the purple and green silks rode lightly as he continued warming up his horse. Gabby'd been on the circuit for years, and on Preacher a number of times this summer. Merv had told Jonas that Gabby thought Preacher had great potential—one of the best three-year-olds he'd ever been on.

Jonas and his family watched as the field of eight horses made their way toward the starting gate at the head of the track. As soon as they reached the portable gate with its twelve individual stalls, the track handlers began leading the horses in and slamming a metal gate behind them. A spring-loaded gate in front would be released by the starter when all of the horses were in. Preacher stood in number four—the middle of the pack. Not the best position, but maybe he could break away fast, before he got bumped in the traffic, Jonas hoped.

"They're in line … AND THEY'RE OFF!" the loud-speaker screamed. "It's Grady's Gold on the inside to a quick lead, Frosty Cattis in second, and Main Man Martin is third. Nicole's Babe is fourth, and Sweet Svensson on the outside is fifth."

"Come on, Preacher, break out!" Jonas heard himself yelling. "Get out of the pack and move inside!"

"It's Grady's Gold still in the lead, followed by Main Man Martin, and Nicole's Babe starting to gain. Coming into the turn, it's 1, 3, and 4."

"Go, Preacher, go!" Becca was screaming beside Jonas while E.J., in Jonas's arms, had his chubby little hands over his ears. "Number 4, that's Midnight Preacher, is coming on strong!" the announcer's voice raised a level. "He's in second, and gaining fast. It's still Grady's Gold in the lead, with Nicole's Babe in second and Sweet Svensson in third."

Jonas's heart quickened as he saw the coal black horse gain on the bay stallion just ahead of him. The thundering pack wasn't far behind them, but it looked to be a two-horse race. Preacher and Grady's Gold.

"Coming down the backstretch, it's Grady's Gold and Midnight Preacher! Three lengths back, Sweet Svensson is holding onto third, and Julia's Child is in fourth! And now Grady's Gold and Midnight Preacher are neck and neck!"

For a moment, Jonas watched as the two horses matched stride for stride on the track across the grassy oval from the grandstand. He wished for the binoculars, but knew better than to try to get them away from the girls. Suddenly, Preacher pushed ahead!

"Go, Preacher!" Jonas hollered into the crowd of noises around him. "Do it now! Go, Preacher, go!"

The eight horses pounded down the backstretch, but only one was running away from the pack in the Thoroughbred Handicap. One horse—a shiny black stallion named Midnight Preacher—ate up the last furlong in deep powerful strides, building distance between him and the others. There was no mistaking the heart and the legacy of this horse. One clear leader rounded the last turn and stretched for home.

"It's Midnight Preacher pulling away from the field! Midnight Preacher has taken control! He's going to win this one going away!" the announcer cried.

"Yes, Preacher, yes!" Jonas yelled. "You did it! You did it!"

Preacher crossed the electronic finish line, and the Bontrager family exploded. "Preacher! Preacher!" the girls screamed, jumping up and down on the bleachers. Even E.J. was clapping his hands and yelling "Peech-er! Peech-er!" Sue Ann stepped over and put her arms around Jonas, her dark eyes bright and her cheeks flushed with excitement. "He did it, Jonas! Did you see that?"

Jonas couldn't stop laughing and smiling. What a horse! What a race!

"Excuse me, sir," a man standing beside Jonas interjected. "I can't help but see how excited your family is about that horse winning. Do you know the horse or the owners?"

"Yeah, we know the horse," Jonas smiled.

"And we used to own him," Becca piped up. "I've ridden him!"

"Oh, my goodness!" the man exclaimed. "Why'd you ever sell him?"

"It's a long story," Jonas said, signaling Becca with his

eyes. "He's a winner though, isn't he?"

"The way he finished that race, he's gonna go places," the man said.

"Yeah, I do believe you're right."

❖ ❖ ❖

Late that evening, when the family was getting ready for bed at the retreat center, Becca asked Jonas about the teenage girl they'd seen walking Preacher to cool him down after the race.

"She works at the stable," Jonas said. "In fact, I think she helped break Preacher."

"How old is she?" Becca wondered, unrolling her sleeping bag on the floor.

"Oh, I don't know. Maybe 16, 17."

"Does she always get to take care of Preacher?"

"A lot of the time, probably."

Becca didn't say anything more as she settled into her bag. Jonas helped Lydianne into hers, and Sue Ann was putting pajamas on E.J.

"Dad," Becca said.

"Yes?"

"When I'm 16, I'm going to Indiana to take care of Preacher."

"You think so?"

"Yep."

"Well, we'll see about that. Good-night, Becca."

"Good-night, Dad. Night-night, Mom."

THE END

The Authors

Husband-and-wife authors Maynard Knepp and Carol Duerksen share their farm between Goessel and Hillsboro, Kansas, with exchange students and a variety of animals. Maynard grew up Amish near Yoder, Kansas, and provided the inspiration and information for this book. He works for a tree care business.

Carol is a full-time freelance writer. She edits *With*, a Christian youth magazine; and writes Sunday school curriculum, among other projects. Maynard and Carol are active members of the Tabor Mennonite Church.

The Illustrator

Susan Bartel has illustrated several books and many magazine stories. She lives with her husband in Colorado Springs, Colorado.

OTHER BOOKS FROM
WILLOWSPRING DOWNS

JONAS SERIES

The Jonas Series was the brainchild of Maynard Knepp, a popular speaker on the Amish culture who grew up in an Amish family in central Kansas. Knepp and his wife Carol Duerksen, a freelance writer, collaborated to produce their first book, *Runaway Buggy*, released in October, 1995. The resounding success of that book encouraged them to continue, and the series grew to four books within 18 months. The books portray the Amish as real people who face many of the same decisions, joys and sorrows as everyone else, as well as those that are unique to their culture and tradition. Written in an easy-to-read style that appeals to a wide range of ages and diverse reader base — from elementary age children to folks in their 90s, from dairy farmers to PhDs — fans of the Jonas Series are calling it captivating, intriguing, can't-put-it-down reading.

RUNAWAY BUGGY

This book sweeps the reader into the world of an Amish youth trying to find his way "home." Not only does *Runaway Buggy* pull back a curtain to more clearly see a group of people, but it intimately reveals the heart of one of their sons struggling to become a young man all his own.

HITCHED

With *Hitched*, the second installment in the Jonas Series, the reader struggles with Jonas as he searches for the meaning of Christianity and tradition, and feels his bewilderment as he recognizes that just as there are Christians who are not Amish, there are Amish who are not Christians.

PREACHER

Book Three in the Jonas Series finds Jonas Bontrager the owner of a racehorse named Preacher, and facing dilemmas that only his faith can explain, and only his faith can help him endure.

BECCA

The fourth book in the Jonas Series invites readers to see the world through the eyes of Jonas Bontrager's 16-year-old daughter Becca, as she asks the same questions her father did, but in her own fresh and surprising ways.

SKYE SERIES

A spin-off of the much-loved Jonas Series, the Skye Series follows Jonas Bontrager's daughter Becca as she marries and becomes the mother of twin daughters, Angela and Skye. While Angela rests on an inner security of who she is and what life is about, Skye's journey takes her to very different places and situations. Through it all, she holds tightly to one small red piece of security—a bandanna her Amish grandfather gave her as a child.

TWINS

In the first book of the Skye Series, Becca and her husband Ken become the parents of twin daughters through very unusual circumstances—circumstances that weave the twins' lives together even as they are pulled apart by their separate destinies.

AFFAIR OF THE HEART

Not long after rock star Skye Martin settles into the Wellsford Amish community, the tongues begin to wag. She's been seen a lot lately with Ezra Yoder, an Amish man who always did seem to have secrets of his own.

SWEDE

A Swedish exchange student hopes to enjoy life in the sun and surf of California, but instead finds himself on the Kansas wheatfield prairies, meeting an old Amishman called Dawdi, and falling in love with a beautiful Mennonite girl.

Slickfester Dude Tells Bedtime Stories
Life Lessons from our Animal Friends

by Carol Duerksen (& Slickfester Dude)

WillowSpring Downs is not only a publishing company — it's also a 120-acre piece of paradise in central Kansas that's home to a wide assortment of animals. Slickfester Dude, a black cat with three legs that work and one that doesn't, is one of those special animals. In a unique book that only a very observant cat could write, Slickfester Dude tells Carol a bedtime story every night — a story of life among the animals and what it can mean for everyone's daily life. This book will delight people from elementary age and up because the short stories are told in words that both children and adults can understand and take to heart. Along with strong, sensitive black and white story illustrations, the book includes Slickfester Dude's Photo Album of his people and animal friends at WillowSpring Downs.

Order Form

BOOKS

Runaway Buggy	____@ $9.95=$	_____
Hitched	____@ $9.95=$	_____
Preacher	____@ $9.95=$	_____
Becca	____@ $9.95=$	_____
Twins	____@ $9.95=$	_____
Affair of the Heart	____@ $9.95=$	_____
Swede	____@ $9.95=$	_____
Slickfester Dude Tells Bedtime Stories	____@ $9.95=$	_____

MERCHANDISE TOTAL $_____

Add $3 shipping/handling $_____
    if ordering one item

Add $5 shipping/handling $_____
    if ordering two or more items

TOTAL ENCLOSED $_____

Make check or money order payable to WillowSpring Downs and mail, along with this order form, to:

> WillowSpring Downs
> 1582 Falcon
> Hillsboro, KS 67063

Name _____

Address _____

City _____

State/Province_____ Zip/Postal Code _____

Phone # _____

For information on speaking engagements and books
Call **1-888-551-0973** and leave your phone number, or e-mail us at:
willowspringdowns@juno.com
Fax: 620-367-8218